ANGEL GRACE

By
J.E. Taylor

J.E. TAYLOR
SUPERNATURAL SUSPENSE
& DARK FANTASY AUTHOR

ANGEL GRACE

When the devil ripped my angelic father's head
off, that was just the start of my bad day.
Walking in on my girlfriend screwing someone
else made it officially the worst day of my life.
And left one hell of a scar on my already
damaged soul.

But it keeps getting worse.

You see, Lucifer wants my meatsuit. He wants
my natural powers. He wants Armageddon. And
he wants it now. But in order to get that, I have
to say yes.

And the devil throws a lot of nasty tricks my way
to get me to yield. But I can't give in, even if it
means watching everyone I love die.

If I cave, the entire world will burn.

Chapter 1

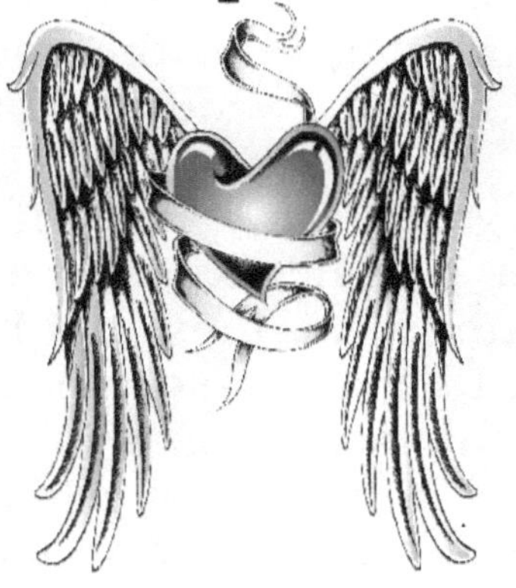

I STARED OUT THE window at the horror in front of me. The shrill cry of the baby in the background couldn't pull my attention away, not with the fight to the death unfolding on the snow-covered lawn. The battle between my father and Lucifer raged, dredging up a white flurry around the two angels. My heartbeat rammed my throat, drawing my breath in fast pants of anxiety as I watched each mighty blow.

Red splattered white and I bellowed at the vision of my father's head in the demon's grip. My palms banged against the cold windowpane as blood rained down on my father's wings. Even my brother couldn't break through the devastation layering my heart, and my inability to influence Damian's actions just added to my frustration.

A second trembling cry broke through the blackness shrouding me, and I glanced at my brother. Tom's gaze was glued to the scene outside while tears slowly tracked down his cheeks. His lips pressed together, and he grieved in silence, but I felt the darkness grip his heart as surely as it griped my own. Tom's saving grace was the baby in his arms. The child tempered his reaction and the cry of disdain coming from the baby's lips pulled both our eyes to the swaddled bundle; Damian's first born.

I tore my gaze away and refocused on the macabre scene outside. Lucifer decimated three angels in a matter of minutes, and I wondered how, in God's name, Damian could conquer the bastard. Damian held the same vengeful expression my reflection carried and my jaw clenched. My hands followed suit, and my nails drove painful welts into my palms. When Damian's hand shot toward Lucifer's chest, I commanded it to smash through the angel's unbreakable skin. I willed Damian the strength to shatter bone and rip the devil's heart out.

Power leaped from the center of my being like a bolt of lightning and surprise raked through my form when Damian's hand came into view, holding a beating heart. And then Damian did the unthinkable: he took a bite of the bloody muscle. Disgust filtered through me, burning through the horror, and my hand shot over my mouth, clamping down control over my roiling stomach.

The moment the last piece of the bastard's heart disappeared into Damian's mouth, the heavens opened, and a blinding light encompassed him, dropping Damian to his knees. I stared at the man in the midst of the heavenly glow, wondering if the angel grace effect would last. Tom gasped at the spectacle, and I traded a glance with him before refocusing on the bloodied winter scene. The glow faded, and Damian climbed to his feet. The fury etched into his features made me want to shrink away from the glass and I couldn't imagine being the recipient of such wrath.

A blast leaped from Damian, enveloping Lucifer, leaving only torched earth where the devil had stood.

Damian took an unsteady step backwards, reaching for the gazebo post for support as he stared at the same blackened spot. His gaze met mine, and he put the back of his wrist to his lips, paling under the bright moonlight. When Damian finally started toward the house, his gait was steady and he ignored the severed heads sprinkling his path.

As the former vampire passed by my father's head, my gaze locked on the vacant eyes staring at the sky. Anguish encompassed me, numbing my body, and I dropped my chin to my chest, ignoring the birthing process happening less than ten feet away.

I didn't want to be here.

I didn't want to know there were such dark creatures crawling top-side.

I didn't want to experience this type of devastation again.

What I wanted was Sandy.

Sandy had always stood by my side, keeping me sane after my sister died and again many years later when we buried my older brother. She held my hand at my father's funeral and again at my mother's. Losing my brother and then my parents so close together nearly undid me, and Tom was no help during that dark period. He was too busy insulating himself from everyone after being kidnapped and tortured by a madman.

Sandy kept me in line when my world nearly fell to pieces. I couldn't help but blame Steve. Even though I knew it was only the proximity to the former FBI agent that got most of my family killed in that small span of time, it still didn't stop me from feeling he caused the catastrophe. The twist I never saw coming was my father becoming Steve's guardian angel. Because of that, I could hear my father through Steve's mind, and hearing his voice tempered my rage, but not the sense of loss.

Sandy helped fill that void. She was there at every turn, even when her parents forbid her from seeing me. I breezed through college in two years instead of four and had to wait for her to graduate. The past two years seemed to stretch forever, but this spring, she would get her diploma and I planned to pop the question the moment she stepped off the podium.

I hadn't seen her since Christmas break and that disaster was still in the forefront of my mind. Her father had refused to let me in the house and, while I could have forced my way in, I didn't; not with Sandy shaking her head and silently pleading for me not to make another scene.

It was the first time she had truly given into her father's will since she'd turned eighteen and it irked the hell out of me. I left her present in the driveway with the keys in the ignition; and I can still hear her father yelling for me to come get the goddamned car as I trudged away from the house.

It wasn't my worst Christmas, but it came close. I hitched home on Christmas Eve, and Sandy and I didn't talk until New Year's, when she was able to find the time to call without her father standing over her shoulder.

This semester had been tough to deal with. Her course load was insane and with a part-time job and an internship, it made it nearly impossible to catch more than a moment with her by phone and no luck at all with seeing her in person. She kept saying she'd let me know when she had a day off, but it'd been close to two weeks since we actually spoke, and all my messages garnered was a quick text response or an equally brief message in my voicemail box.

I stared at the blood-soaked snow and decided spring was too long to wait.

I needed her now.

The wail of a third baby pulled my attention, and I turned in time to see the little girl swaddled and placed on Naomi's chest. Damian rattled off the names of the boys honoring the fallen angels, my father included, and I gave him a nod of thanks. When Damian and Naomi decided on the name Grace, for their little girl, my lips curved into a ghost of a smile.

Chapter 2

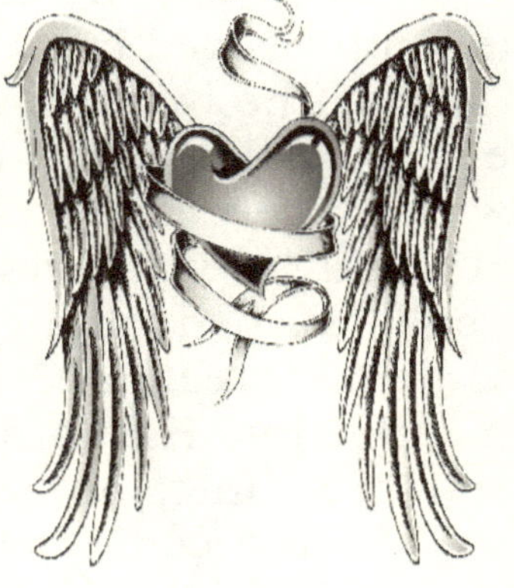

WHEN WE ARRIVED HOME, the feds swarmed around us and the media had already pitched camp outside the gate. I traded a glance with Steve and pulled my keys out of my pocket.

"I'm going to see Sandy." I stepped toward the decimated doors of the garage, ignoring the chaos surrounding our home in Maine.

Steve gave me a nod. "Drive safe," he said before he turned towards his ex-boss, effectively dismissing me.

I didn't envy him; trying to explain the blood-soaked family room and equally stained back yard was going to be difficult and I know the death of his old partner was something that would eat away at him for years. Instead of staying and helping, I bolted, leaving the four of them to clean up the mess. Sliding into my car, I backed it out of the driveway, away from the police and away from the cameras and microphones.

As soon as I hit the highway and the silence descended, the previous night's events hit like a tractor-trailer mowing through a stalled car. My eyes stung and my vision blurred. The road wobbled under the sheen of tears and I swallowed, forcing down the lump wedged in my throat.

"Damn it." I swiped the wetness from my cheeks and pressed the gas pedal, tipping the speedometer into the territory of dangerous. By the time I hit the interstate 84 interchange, my tears had dried up, but my eyes still burned and the emptiness overtaking my soul still threatened.

The rest of the drive into Hartford was quiet, and I concentrated on breathing, on relaxing the coil that had tightened in the center of my chest. My head throbbed as I pulled into the visitor's parking lot outside Sandy's dorm at the University of Hartford. I took a moment and leaned my head on the edge of my steering wheel, trying to get my emotions in check.

I exhaled when I realize I'd been holding my breath and pulled the keys from the ignition, stepping out into the cool night. The slap of cold air cleared my head, and I scanned the parking lot. I really didn't want to have to wait for her in the lobby of her building, or worse, track her down at her job. It took two passes before I located her car and relief settled into my muscles, leaving me unsteady, like I'd had too much to drink. I closed my eyes, willing myself to shake it off.

I was not in the mood for chatting with the resident assistant at the desk while I waited for Sandy to come sign me in, so instead of buzzing in as I had in the past, I silently commanded the doors to open and kept walking past the busy reception desk, like I belonged. No one paid attention to me and I slipped up the stairs, tuning out all thoughts accosting me.

I didn't bother knocking on her door, either, and when the wood swung open, I stopped, frozen in place, with my hand on the handle. Sandy turned from her straddled position and gasped. Neither she, nor the guy she was riding, expected visitors and they certainly did not expect me.

I couldn't move. I just stared, dumbfounded, until my fingers tingled, reminding me I hadn't turned to stone. Reality set in and my heart tumbled to the floor, shriveling to a blackened husk. When I stepped into the room, the door swung behind me and closed with an ominous click.

Sandy pulled the sheet around her, attempting to cover her naked form, and that was the final trigger.

A harsh laugh escaped, one that even I didn't recognize, and I crossed my arms. "So, this is the reason you can't seem to find time for me," I said with a voice that was nothing more than a feral growl, and Sandy's face transformed into a mask of fear.

"Chris. I," Sandy started and turned her back for a minute, but she didn't disengage from the man under her. In fact, I caught the look he traded with her, along with his thoughts, before Sandy turned back. The betrayal ran deeper than just a sordid fuck. It involved feelings, and when she met my glare, I knew it was over.

The ache to strike out ballooned and my fists curled as the fury overrode all senses.

"Don't," she yelled, twisting, so she protected the bastard who stole her heart. Both her hands came up, and her wide eyes shot to my soul, fracturing what little reserve I had left.

I snarled and clenched my teeth, letting the fury snake through my body, poisoning my blood until my skin burned. "You're fucking kidding me. You're protecting that shithead?"

Sandy knew exactly what I was capable of, and her fear blanketed me, stopping me from letting loose. Tears filled her eyes, and she finally slid off him, taking the space next to him on the mattress. She pulled the sheet over her exposed flesh and nodded. "His name is Josh," she said, like that made all the difference in the world.

"You don't need to protect me." Josh sat up.

I twitched, shooting a concentrated blast in his direction. Josh slammed back on the mattress with an audible 'oof'. His hands flew to his throat, clawing at my invisible strangle hold. The fear in his eyes sparked a smile, and I suddenly understood the rush my father always spoke about. He was right. There's nothing quite like scaring the shit out of someone.

"Chris, stop," Sandy yelled, breaking through my concentration.

I let go and Josh gasped for air, his features now holding the same layers of fear as Sandy's.

"What the hell are you?" Josh whispered.

"I'm your worst fucking nightmare," I said, borrowing my father's favorite warning, and then shifted my gaze to Sandy. "Why?" I asked, because I couldn't figure out what this chump had that I didn't.

"I didn't plan on this," she said, wrapping the sheet tighter. "It just happened."

"Do you have any clue how many girls I've fought off over the years?" I started and stopped, shifting my stance and glaring at the floor. "How many times I said no because of you?" I finished and met her teary stare.

"Please," she whispered.

"Please, what?" I snapped. "Don't kill him? Don't make a scene? What?"

"I should have told you," she said.

"Damned right." I crossed my arms again. When she did not explain further, I pressed my lips together against every callous response. When I was certain I wouldn't dig into her and had a solid grip on the need to strike out, I pointed an accusing finger in Josh's direction. "That's what you want?"

She nodded. "Yes," she said in an almost inaudible voice.

Disbelief swept through me. After all, I was CJ Ryan, heir to billions, a fucking Mensa-level genius, and I harbored enough psychic power to destroy the universe. I could offer her the world.

What the hell could he offer her?

The truth almost knocked the wind out of me. Josh could help patch up the rift Sandy had with her father. But knowing the one thing Josh brought to the equation that I couldn't, didn't erase the pain.

"Really? After all these years? This is how it ends?"

She looked at the floor and then back. "Yes."

"Fuck you," I snarled and leveled a deadly glare. It took everything I had to turn and walk out of her room without unleashing hell. A door opened when I was halfway down the hall.

"Chris?"

Her voice stopped me, but I refused to turn, not with her thoughts parading through my mind.

"I'm sorry," she whispered. "This isn't the way..." she trailed off and every muscle in my body stiffened.

I didn't need to ask the questions a normal man would ask. I got everything I needed to know from Josh's thoughts and now Sandy's weren't hidden anymore, either.

"I know you can see," she whispered, and I glanced over my shoulder.

I could see everything that led up to this moment. Everything. The conflict, the fucking love she felt for that deadbeat. Everything.

And everything crushed my heart to a pulp.

"You'd better shut your mind off, because if I get any more of your insane narrative, I'm going to make this entire building implode," I said, and I meant it. I needed to get away now, before I lost control of the raging beast.

I didn't wait; the minute I hit the stairs, I was in full flight mode and the cold air slapped my face a few moments later. I leaned against the cool bricks, counting breaths until my gaze fell on the student parking lot... and her car.

The car *I* bought her and the anger leaped out before I could stop it.

The explosion echoed off the buildings, and I blinked at the damage. Her car was in pieces, burned metal littered the ground, and the cars surrounding hers were now in flames. It felt good to destroy, and I exhaled, letting out a laugh, thankful that losing control only annihilated a car and not the entire university campus. I forced my feet to move forward toward the adjoining visitor's lot.

My car couldn't outrun the onslaught of fury. It couldn't perform fast enough, not through the side streets of Hartford, and certainly not on the highway. When lights and sirens appeared in my rearview mirror, I growled under my breath and considered doing the same damage I did back at Sandy's dorm. The only thing that stopped me was the damned moral compass my mother instilled in me. I have the same high regard for life that she had, and Steve, being a federal agent, just ingrained it further into me. It's the one thing that separated me from my father and despite the disdain careening through me, I slowed my car, pulling over in the emergency lane and dropped the gears into neutral, setting the parking brake before running my hands through my hair.

I knew just how deep in shit I was.

The cop took his time, radioing in the license plate before he finally approached the driver's side door.

I glanced out the window, meeting the officer's questioning gaze.

"Do you know how fast you were going?"

I knew. The needle was buried beyond the 120 mark and I considered saying no, but I nodded instead. My jaw ached from being clenched, and I kept my lips closed against the flurry of sarcastic responses that begged to leap forth.

His features hardened. "Please step out of the car." He straightened, stepping away from the door with his hand on the butt of his gun.

"I haven't been drinking." I glared out the window.

"Please step out of the car."

"Fine," I muttered and stepped out.

"Please put your hands on the car." The officer's tone was now stony.

I had been hauled into police stations more than once and knew the routine, but this time, I was silent, unlike the times in Maine and New Hampshire when I was younger and rebelling against the world with Tom.

After the officer patted me down, he stepped back, assessing me. "Please step to the back of the car.," he said after a few minutes of silence.

I stepped to the back and waited for the sobriety test instructions. Walk in a straight line, touch your nose, and stand on one foot. I did everything the officer instructed until the officer crossed his arms.

"Where's the fire?" he finally asked.

A tractor-trailer zoomed by, creating a breeze that ruffled through my hair, and I met the officer's stare. "Ever catch your girlfriend in bed with another guy?" I asked, and the cop's eyebrows rose. "I guess I let it get the better of me."

The officer rubbed his chin and chuckled. "That's an understatement, son. I'm supposed to haul your ass in for the speed you were going."

I leaned against the car and shrugged. "Do what you gotta do."

I really didn't care. With what had transpired in the last forty-eight hours, a little jaunt in jail wasn't the worst thing in the world, and I almost laughed at the irony.

The officer studied me closer, his eyes narrowing as a new thought dawned, and I rolled my eyes.

"I wasn't trying to kill myself," I said before the officer's thought fully formed. "I'm angry, and I took it out on the road. If you have to arrest me, go ahead. I won't give you any shit."

The officer pressed his lips together; his internal debate broadcasting to me as if he was talking aloud. I waited, trying not to show my impatience or irritation at the pity blooming in the officer.

I knew his decision before he opened his mouth and my muscles relaxed.

"I'm going to give you a break," he said. "But you have to give me your word that you won't tear out of here like a bat out of hell."

I allowed a smile to form and bit down on the first snide remark that entered my mind. Instead, I nodded and said, "Thanks."

"I've been there," the cop added and snapped the ticket book closed. "Just keep it reasonable."

I turned and climbed into the driver's seat, squashing the urge to spin gravel at the squad car.

The officer gave me a pass instead of doing his job, which was rare, and judiciousness won out. I started the ignition and pulled onto the road, bottling up the anger.

Chapter 3

THE HOUSE WAS QUIET when I walked in. The drone of the television filtered from the back room and I slapped a lock on my thoughts, guarding them against Steve's unfiltered mind probe. He looked up when I stepped into the family room and his brow scrunched, but I just kept walking, right out into the backyard, crossing through the bloody grass where Damian had annihilated a group of hellhounds, to the rock wall at the far end of the lawn.

I stood, staring out at the churning Atlantic, my jaw clenching and unclenching in concert with my hands. The anger overwhelmed me, and my eyes darted for a source to aim at. Nothing suitable for destroying entered my field of vision and I let out a guttural roar, slamming my fist down on the flat slate rock.

Pain snaked up my arm, and I straightened, pulling my fist to my chest, blinking back the sudden mist covering my eyes. The agony of splintered bones tempered the fury and my chin dropped to my chest.

A hand descended on my shoulder, and I turned, expecting to see Steve, but Jennifer stood at my side. Her green eyes were soft with concern, enough so that when she pulled me into a hug, I allowed it.

"Sandy called?"

"She was worried," Jennifer whispered in my ear.

"I blew her car up." I laid my forehead on Jennifer's shoulder. The admission opened up the wall I'd built around the pain, and it nearly bowed me over. I was so consumed with anger that the reality of losing Sandy hadn't registered until now. Tears started, and she just held me, stroking my back and whispering 'shh' as I cried.

I shifted, knocking my hand against her, and winced before pulling away. "I think I broke my hand," I whispered, and she dropped her gaze to the swollen appendage before giving me a nod.

"I'd venture to guess you did, too," she said.

I wiped the sleeve of my jacket across my face, mopping up the damp tears, before I sniffled and glanced out at the ocean.

"Steve will fix it when you're ready to come in." She gave my shoulder a soft pat and stepped toward the house.

"Jenn?"

She turned, meeting my gaze.

"Did she say why?"

"No, honey. She just said you two broke up and she was worried about you."

"Broke up. That's what she's calling it." I laughed and shook my head, turning toward the water. "It feels more like she put a butcher knife in my chest."

"CJ," Jennifer started, and I glanced over my shoulder.

"I walked in on her fucking another guy."

Jennifer took a step back. Her jaw dropped open before she recovered and stepped closer.

"Yeah, that's the same look I think I wore when I first saw them." I turned back to the ocean. "It felt good to let the power rip. I'm sure some cars are probably still burning."

"Did you..."

"No, I didn't hurt anyone," I cut her off. "I wanted to, but I didn't."

Her hand squeezed my shoulder, and I detested the fact that her show of compassion brought forth more tears. I squeezed my injured hand, welcoming the sharp pain instead of the ballooning agony in the center of my soul.

"Come on, let's have Steve look at that," she said, and I let her lead me back into the house.

Steve's gaze dropped to my hand. "Looks like the slate won."

His response surprised me, and I snorted. "Better my hand than the entire East Coast."

"True." Steve approached me.

I wasn't sure I wanted Steve to fix the broken bones with his miracle healing power. "Maybe I should just go to the hospital." I flexed my hand again, wincing. The pain dulled everything, and I rather liked the diversion.

"Excuse me?" Steve said, stopping short.

I met his gaze but didn't say a word. Instead, I just curled my fist and clamped my jaw tight, sending a smile in Steve's direction.

The silent showdown was broken by the ring of the doorbell. Jennifer traded a glance with Steve before she headed out of the room to answer the door.

Steve reached for my hand, and I stepped back, knocking his hand out of range. Footfalls echoed through the house, pulling our attention to the doorway, and Damian Andreas stepped into view.

"Sorry to interrupt, but I need to grab our stuff from upstairs." Damian hesitated, trading a glance with me. His gaze dropped to my hand and his eyebrows shot up in an amusing arch. "Assuming it's still here." His gaze snapped to Steve.

"The feds left your stuff alone. It's still in the bedroom."

Damian started across the room and slowed to a stop before he got to the stairs. "I'm sorry about your father." His gaze locked on the floor.

Damian's remorse drifted over me. His sense of loss for not only his relatives but for mine as well, made my voice stick in my throat. Instead of responding, I squeezed my fist tighter, sucking air through my teeth.

Damian's gaze shot from the floor to me. "What the fuck are you doing?" he asked, echoing Steve's exact thoughts.

"My girlfriend broke up with me today."

"So, you thought smashing the bones in your hand would somehow make the heartache go away?" Damian asked, filling in the blanks accurately, like he had a special line directly into my mind.

I glared at Damian. "Get out of my head."

"I'm not *in* your head." Damian said. "Besides, it doesn't work for long." He pointed his chin toward my hand before disappearing up the stairs.

"What do you know?" I whispered under my breath.

"A lot more than you." The answer drifted down to me from upstairs.

Steve crossed to the window, pulling the curtain back. When he turned, irritation was written in the lines on his face and he pressed his lips together, waiting for Damian to return.

"You stole a car?" he snapped when Damian stepped into the family room.

Damian shrugged as if it's no big deal. "I couldn't exactly rent or buy without ID." He held up his wallet before tucking it into his pocket. "I'm going to return it," he mumbled and shifted, dropping his gaze.

"There was a car in the garage at the cottage."

"I know. The battery was dead, and it's too small for three car seats. Before Naomi and the kids can leave the hospital, I need a vehicle that will be big enough. I already found what I want, but I didn't have my ID or bank cards on me, so I was shit out of luck."

I couldn't help but smile. Damian's justifications seemed valid, but that little tick over Steve's left eye engaged, and I knew he was pissed.

"You ever hear of a phone?"

Damian glanced at me for help, and I raised my hands, giving him the 'you made this bed yourself' look, and he pressed his lips into a thin line, focusing back on Steve.

"I didn't want to inconvenience you anymore than I already had," he finally said and started for the door.

"CJ, why don't you go with him and make sure he gets that car back to where it belongs," Steve said and turned towards me. He used my shock as his opening and closed the distance before my brain restarted, but it was too late, he planted a quick kiss on my temple and the healing vibe slid from the point of impact, down my arm and into my hand in a progression of pins and needles I was helpless to stop.

"Damn it." I sent a glare his way as a crushing pain surrounded my hand. That's the thing about his healing power. It always hurts like a motherfucker.

He grinned and shrugged, waving me toward the door. Sometimes I hated the man.

"I wasn't put here to make your life easy," he said to my internal commentary.

I bit down on the automatic 'Fuck you' his comment elicited, but his smirk told me he heard it, anyway.

"Go keep Damian from getting into any more trouble, will you?" He pointed to the door.

"I don't..." Damian started, and Steve sent a glare in his direction, silencing him, but I heard the unspoken 'need a babysitter' in his mind.

A layer of irritation surfaced, and I knew exactly what Steve was doing. It wasn't Damian that needed babysitting. It was me.

"Damned straight," Steve said. "You need a diversion." He looked pointedly at my hand and then back to my eyes, using my own thoughts against me. "I figure helping our new friend find a car and a place to live might occupy your mind for a little while."

From the look on Damian's face, he was about as happy as I was about this, but to his credit, he kept his mouth shut.

Chapter 4

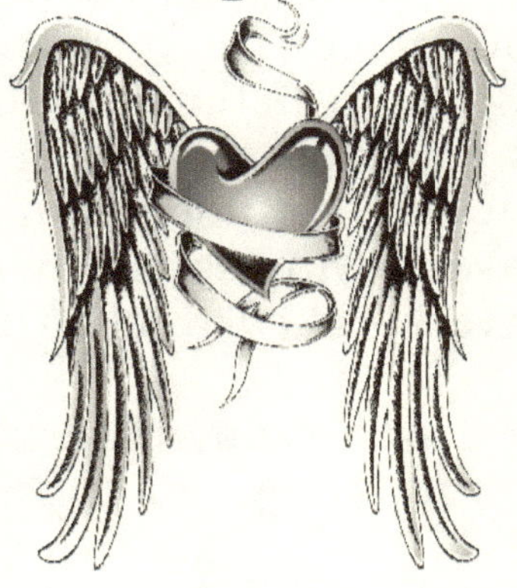

ROUTE 4 WAS QUIET at this time of the night, and I stared at the houses as we passed by. Damian was trying to figure out how the hell he and Naomi were going to deal with triplets. Just the ordeal at the hospital was harrowing for him, but the thought of succumbing to a family car brought forth a "humph."

I couldn't help but chuckle. An ancient vampire reduced to a minivan. It was laughable, and he sent a glare in my direction.

"What happened?" Damian asked, turning the tables on me.

"I walked in on her fucking someone else."

Damian had the decency to sigh. "That's rough."

"Yeah, fifteen years out the window like that." I snapped my fingers.

"First love," he whispered and nodded. "That's always the one that kicks your ass." He sent a smile at me. "Be thankful she wasn't your cousin."

I burst out laughing, and Damian met my gaze before I realized he was serious. I choked off my laughter and raise an eyebrow. "Your cousin?"

"You've got the memories. Take a look."

Yeah, I had his memories; twenty-five hundred-years' worth of memories. It wasn't as easy as sifting through one lifetime, but I found the references, and got another viewing of her death at the hands of Lucifer. A shudder ran through me. At least I didn't have to witness Sandy's death. I'm not sure I could have handled that on the heels of my father.

Perhaps Steve was right; hanging with Damian may just be the thing to put my life into perspective.

It was Damian's turn to laugh. "My life won't give you perspective. Nightmares, maybe, but not perspective." He glanced in my direction before taking the exit for Brooksfield. After a few more turns, he pulled into the mall parking lot and came to a stop in one of the farthest parking spots.

"Time to walk." He tucked the keys under the corner of the carpeting on the driver's side floor before opening his door. The wind whipped through the car, and I stepped out into the brutal New Hampshire chill. It was colder than it had been the other night. Either that or my adrenaline had kept me warm during the run from the devil.

"The hospital is this way." Damian nodded toward the road we just drove in on.

I followed him with my hands stuffed in my pockets and my chin tucked into my coat. I wished I'd had the forethought of grabbing a hat, and by the time we got a football length away from the car, I thought my ears were going to fall off from the frigid bite.

Damian sent a sideways glare in my direction.

"It's fucking cold." My voice rose with defensiveness.

"You live in Northern New England. What the hell do you expect this time of year?"

"York is not this cold," I muttered and scrunched my shoulders to cover whatever exposed skin I could.

"The Rockies in the dead of winter is cold. This is balmy in comparison." He continued walking, ignoring my grumbling.

I followed in silence, wondering what the hell was wrong with me. I normally didn't mind the cold. I normally didn't whine. Hell, I normally didn't have the emotional spectrum of a teenage girl.

Damian snorted laughter and looked over his shoulder.

"Fuck you," I muttered under my breath, but he had every cause to laugh. I was a fucking mess. Aggravation snuck in like a cat burglar, at first undetected, but then the silent stalk got sloppy, jumbling my nerves. My eyes stung from more than just the wind, and finally Damian stopped and faced me.

"Think of it this way. There's gotta be something better out there for you."

I stopped and stared at him. "Did you ever have anyone you loved walk away from you?" I tried to decipher his memories. I didn't think that was the case and from the slow shake of his head, he confirmed it.

"It's a little different when they decide you aren't what they want." Bitterness snaked in alongside the aggravation, and I clenched my jaw, blinking away the remnants of mist from my eyes.

"Loss is loss. Mine was just a little more... permanent," he said.

I glared at him, even though his tone wasn't snarky or sarcastic.

"Look, everything happens for a reason." He turned and started walking again. "It took me a long time to accept that," he added when I caught up.

We walked in silence and while I agreed everything happens for a reason, losing Sandy wasn't something I had been prepared for. In some ways, death would have been easier to accept. At least that didn't bruise the ego.

I glanced at Damian and realized I couldn't hear his thoughts.

He smiled at my revelation. "Frustrating, isn't it?" He focused on the building rising from just beyond the trees. "I can't always hear you, either." His brow creased.

The silence hung between us, but it was now layered with the thought-creep of the hospital inhabitants. "We're almost there." He resumed a faster pace.

A sudden urgency gripped me, and I caught up with him, my feet matching his near sprinting pace. I glanced in his direction, and he had the same trepidation carved into his features as I had in the pit of my stomach. I focused on the thoughts and the word tiger surfaced.

I didn't wait for Damian. I turned my sprint into a full-fledged speed contest. The limited experience I had with Naomi and her stellar ability to change into a ferocious tiger had a direct correlation to demons. And if there were demons in the hospital, it meant Grace was in danger.

The air shifted, and a shadow blocked the bright moon overhead. I dodged around an oak trunk and broke out of the tree line before a talon wrapped around my waist. Air sucked out of my lungs as I was lifted off the ground by a giant hawk. We soared above the parking lot, landing on the roof of the hospital. The talon released and before I had a moment to process what just happened, Damian stood beside me, scanning the rooftop for an access door.

"Dude."

He turned toward me and his gaze traveled beyond me. "Door." He pointed and then headed that way. I followed, still unsteady from the experience. I'm not sure Damian knew he transitioned either until he pulled the door open and sent a glare at me.

"We can discuss my ability after we get rid of the demons. Talking our way in would have only wasted time and they're beyond trying tranquilizers. Now, they're talking about killing the tiger."

"Shit," I said, and we took the stairs as fast as possible. Halfway down, Damian reached for the door, bursting into the maternity ward where a collection of officers were plotting how to take down the rabid tiger in the nursery.

Damian scanned the area, his gaze landing on the glass separating the nursery from the rest of the maternity ward. A nurse had her back pressed to the glass, and a tiger stalked back and forth between the nurse and the bassinets. If anyone had been paying attention, they would have understood the tiger was in protection mode, not attack mode.

The nurse took a step forward and the giant cat snarled, swiping a clawed paw in her direction, sending the nurse back into the glass. I exchanged a glance with Damian.

Distaste colored his features and my nose itched with the stench of sulfur filling the ward. The nurse wasn't the only demon on site, and I turned, facing the crowd behind us. At least a half a dozen police officers stared back and their eyes glimmered, revealing the red eyes of demon possession. The others still focused on the hospital schema laid out on the table and beyond the cops were frightened parents and hospital staff.

I glanced over my shoulder, giving Damian a nod. *I got this; you go take care of that bitch.*

Be careful. His thought echoed in my mind, and he started toward the nursery. I turned, just as one of the normal officers called out to Damian to stop.

"He'll be okay," I said, and the demons behind the officer grinned.

Demonic voices filled my head.

Lucifer has plans for you.

I stared at them, and a chill settled over me. What the fuck does the devil want from me?

A smile was the only response, that and the shift of gazes from me to Damian and the nursery beyond. I'm a smart man and my hands curled into fists. If the devil thought he could use me to get to Naomi and Grace, he had another think coming.

Laughter echoed in my head, and I ground my teeth, tempering the need to demolish everything in my path.

"Sir," another officer called, pulling my attention away from hell's collection in the hallway and over my shoulder toward Damian. He had already crossed the distance and stood on the hallway side of the glass case, behind the back of the demonic nurse. He didn't turn, but his reflection in the glass told me enough. He was gearing up and when his gaze met mine, I started counting.

When I hit three, the roll of power expanded from the two of us like a tidal wave, popping overhead lights, and turning demons and their human suits to dust, including the bitch in the nursery. The maternity ward dropped into the black and frightened murmurs echoed on the tile hallway.

It only took a moment before the generator engaged and the red hue of emergency lights bathed the area. I turned toward the nursery. The door next to the window stood open and Damian's back faced us. Arms wrapped around his waist and the stunned quiet broke with the wail of infants. Other than the two of them and a room full of crying babies, nothing else stirred.

The police converged on the open door.

"Where's the tiger?" someone asked, and Damian glanced toward the voice behind him.

"I don't know." He pulled the sleeve of his jacket up, showing the hospital bracelet that gave him access to his children. "My wife's been in here the whole time. She texted me while you guys did shit," he added, turning so they could see Naomi.

The glare he sent at the trooper was enough to pull a smile to my lips, but I pressed them together, staunching the grin. Radios squawked, and they began the search for the missing terror.

"You let that beast out of the room?" the sergeant approached the nursery door, his aggravation making his lips non-existent. "Do you know how much damage a tiger can cause?"

Damian planted a kiss on Naomi's forehead and released his hold on her, turning on the cop. "Would you have preferred letting it snack on the infants?" He waved his hand towards the collection of cribs. This time, a high-pitched laugh escaped from my lips.

Frantic parents filtered into the room, and Damian lifted two fingers, beckoning me into the room.

"I'm taking my wife and children out of here right now." He showed the matching hospital bracelets that allowed him and Naomi access to their kids, and without further conversation, he grabbed Grace and handed her to me. Michael went into Naomi's arms, and he gathered up Gabriel last. He stepped toward the door and rethought his plan, turning and grabbing the three diaper bags sitting under each bassinet.

I followed the two of them with the baby snug in my arms. "Guys, we can't take the babies outside in the cold," I said, and Damian slowed to a stop before we got to the elevator.

"Fuck," he whispered.

I guess I had been designated the voice of reason because the two of them turned to me like I could magically conjure up a car and three infant seats at this time of night. The head nurse intervened, blocking the path out and tried to herd us back into Naomi's maternity room.

"Can you go get us wheels?" Damian asked in exasperation.

I laughed. I didn't mean to, but I couldn't help it. His request was ludicrous.

"Do I look like Harry fucking Potter?" I asked, and for the first time since we stepped onto this ward, his lips twitched into what I assumed was a smirk.

"Fine." Damian allowed the nurse to escort us to the room. As soon as the three of us were alone and the bassinets were lined along the wall with the triplets inside, I turned to leave.

"Where are you going?" Damian asked.

"I'm going to the lake. Why?" I paused at the door. Damian's doubt and unease stretched across the room, and I crossed my arms. "Dude, I'm not staying here." I had no interest in babysitting all night.

"Just keep watch for a little while. We both need some sleep before the babies wake up again, okay?" he asked.

I glanced at Naomi. She was already curled up on the bed, her eyes at half-mast, and her breathing slowing. In a matter of seconds, she was asleep.

"Give me a few minutes." I slipped out of the room. I wanted to be sure demons didn't get close again and headed to the cafeteria. I gathered a half-dozen saltshakers and brought them back to the room.

Damian's eyebrows rose as I trailed salt from one wall to the other, creating a line that kept them reasonably safe. I tossed the last shaker to Damian, and he lined the windowsill and the entry to the bathroom.

"I'll guard the room," I said and grabbed the chair that sat at the small kitchenette table, bringing it outside before closing the door and camping out in front of the entrance.

The floor was quiet and maintenance workers went from light fixture to light fixture, replacing blown bulbs. I watched until my eyelids got heavy. I closed my eyes just for a moment.

When my eyelids fluttered open, I stared at a pair of deep amber eyes. Her mouth was moving but nothing computed, and I blinked, glancing around at the dim hallway.

"Wouldn't you be more comfortable lying down?"

Her question broke through the haze, and I looked at her again. "What time is it?"

"A little after four." She stood when I rubbed my eyes.

A yawn caught me off guard and I stretched, meeting her gaze. I had dozed off for a couple of hours, not minutes.

"I'm good," I finally said after I settled back in the chair. The din of thought lowered, and she scanned me from head to toe, her leer filled with carnal thoughts that made me blush. She sent a sweet smile my way and turned back toward the desk.

"Maybe a place to lie down isn't a bad idea," I said, and she glanced over her shoulder, a smile played on her lips.

"There's a couch in the nurse's lounge," she said. "Come on, I'll show you."

I stood and followed her on feet that felt like I was sinking in quicksand. I shook my head, trying to wipe out the cobwebs. She opened the door just wide enough for me to squeeze through, and pointed toward the couch, but she was so close and made the mistake of licking her lips in such a way that jump started my libido.

My gaze moved from her wet lips to her eyes, and I offered the slightest of smiles and closed the door behind me.

"You're not really concerned with me getting rest, are you?" I said.

The blush that filled her cheeks was my answer.

Damn, it felt good to be wanted, and I reached out, lacing my fingers into the soft hair at the nape of her neck, and pulled her to me.

Doubt passed over her features, and then our lips met. The kiss was different, awkward at first, and then we both relaxed, toying with each other. I pulled away, hornier than I had been in a very long time, and I didn't bother asking her name, not with the flurry swirling inside me.

I pulled the clip holding her hair in place and the long honey locks fell over her shoulders and I couldn't help but grin. Her hands had drifted from around my neck to the buttons of my shirt, unclasping them before searching my eyes. Her warm palms traveled up my bare chest and over my shoulders, peeling my shirt off with the motion.

As I stared at the hunger in her gaze, I remembered Tom telling me it was intoxicating as hell. I never paid much attention to it before, but with the way this nurse was looking at me, I understood the power of being the subject of such raw lust. Intoxicating was an understatement, and I pinned her against the wall, covering her pouty lips with mine.

For the first time in my life, I threw caution out the window and gave in to the carnal desire, turning my blood to liquid fire.

The flurry of clothing lined the path from the door to the couch. I don't remember much beyond the overwhelming sensation of pleasure and heat. I opened my eyes to the ceiling and the cold floor beneath me. Her hair fanned out over my chest as her breath heaved in her chest from exertion, in time with mine.

She raised her head and met my gaze.

"Holy shit," she mumbled and smiled.

I laughed and looked at the ceiling, trying to understand how screwing a stranger could be so bogglingly hot. Now I understood why Tom had gone the slut route. It was liberating, but now I had to try to gracefully exit, and I had no idea how to do that.

Her chuckle pulled my attention back and my post-sex euphoria disappeared. Her eyes shimmered red, and all the heat in the room evaporated. I tried to push her off and scramble away, but the demon bitch was stronger than I expected, and her thighs clamped down on my hips.

"I could give you this type of bliss for eternity," she whispered and slipped her finger in her mouth, seductively drawing it out of those crimson lips while grinding her hips into me.

"Jesus," I gasped and let a mental shove loose. She tumbled off me in a reverse somersault before jumping to her feet. I grabbed the throw pillow and held it in front of my privates, and laughter peeled from her throat.

"Modesty? Now?" she asked, her hands falling on her waist while her perky breasts still glistened with sweat.

The fact I fucked a demon, no matter how hot her host was, turned my stomach into a boiling pit of acid.

"I suggest you leave that girl alone," I said. My voice was a hell of a lot steadier than the quaking in my soul.

"Or what?" she said, raising an eyebrow. She stepped closer, and I moved back, my gaze dropping to my clothing behind her. I put my hand out and my underwear levitated in my direction. She grabbed it out of the air, keeping it from me.

"Goddamnit," I whispered.

"I'll leave her alone if you allow me in," she said, still gripping my shorts.

Her comment left me dumbstruck, but my basic instincts were demanding I run as far and as fast as possible. I knew what I was capable of, and apparently, so did Lucifer. Possessing me would give him everything he ever wanted, and this little seduction was meant to take advantage of my emotional weakness, to disarm me into saying yes.

What she was suggesting was inviting Armageddon to the world's door.

Fiery heat crawled across my skin, and I welcomed the burn of anger. It fanned the power inside, coiling it into a tight ball. I dropped the pillow, balling my hands into fists as I stood tall, leveling a glare in her direction meant to sear.

She smiled, misreading my intention.

I let the power loose and the stench of burned hair filled the room, along with ash drifting on a swirl of air. My trunks dropped to the floor, and I crossed, swiping them from the ashes and slid them on before collecting the rest of my clothing.

I stalked back down the hall and slumped into the chair outside the door. Fury coursed through my blood, and I shifted, leaning my head against the wall in back of me. Seducing me was a low blow, and the bitch of it all was, I could still feel the demanding stroke of her hands and the heat of her mouth on me.

As much as I didn't want to admit it, fucking her had felt damned good.

Chapter 5

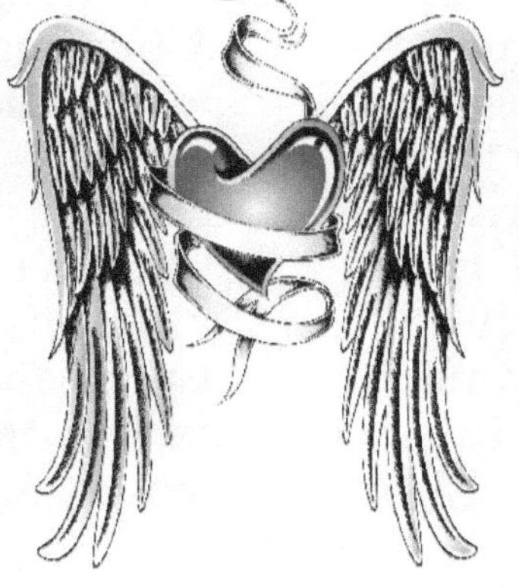

NO ONE ELSE CAME near me. The nursing staff gave me a wide berth as I sat with my arms crossed, giving off a definite 'do not approach' vibe. I remained still and awake, unwilling to put myself in another compromising position. When Damian stepped into the hall at a little after seven, he looked more haggard than I felt.

"I didn't get much sleep." He rubbed his face and covered a lingering yawn. "I need to get us out of here. Today," he added and gave a little shake of his head.

I didn't disagree, especially with the nocturnal encounter. I remained seated.

"You can hang in the room while I'm gone."

"I'm fine right here." I met his gaze. He hesitated, glancing at the cracked door. "If she needs help, she can give me a yell. But, honestly, if I'm out here, I can see what's coming."

He gave me a nod. "Don't let them sweep up the salt, okay?"

"No problem. No one is getting through that door," I said, reassuring him and he turned, heading toward the elevator. "Just make sure you get a car big enough to take me home, too," I called after him. His chuckle filled my head and then he stepped into the elevator and his thoughts blended with the rest of the low-grade din.

As the morning went on, the hallway traffic increased, and with it, so did the tension in my muscles, stretching them taut across my chest like an ever-tightening strap. Every face could be a threat, especially since I wasn't a hundred percent on my game and I finally stood, retreating into the room just to catch a break.

Naomi looked up from the chair with a baby at each breast, and my mouth dropped in surprise. I snapped my gaze to the ceiling and spun back towards the door. Her light laughter at my response made me chuckle as well, but I still didn't turn toward her.

"Good morning," she said, her voice full of exhaustion and humor.

"Morning," I said, still facing the door.

"You don't have to stand in the corner like that," she said.

I took a deep breath, turning toward her again, and my gaze kept dropping to the infants latched on her breasts. "Does that hurt?" I asked, forcing my gaze to hers.

"A little." She offered a shrug. "Can you give me a hand?"

I opened my mouth to speak and then closed it because I didn't want to sound like an idiot. Instead, I just nodded and noticed the trembling in her arms as she shifted. I know breast feeding is supposed to be natural and all that, but for a guy, it makes things... uncomfortable. Especially when it was someone as stunningly beautiful as Naomi.

"Please, take Michael. He needs to be burped."
She struggled to pull the little guy from her right
side.

I paused, and she looked up at me with those
big, brown, expectant eyes. As I crossed the room, I
kept repeating the silent mantra, this is Damian's
wife, and it helped put things into perspective. I
gingerly wrapped my hands around the baby's
midsection and pulled him toward me, painfully
aware of her soft flesh as it brushed against my
knuckles. Sucking sounds filled the air and I
couldn't help it. My gaze dropped from hers to her
fully exposed breast before I turned with the baby
in my arms. Heat filled my cheeks, and I brought
Michael to my shoulder, ignoring the urge to turn
back and ogle.

I got the sense that my behavior amused Naomi.

Cooing in the baby's ear, I rubbed his back and
stepped toward the bed, putting some distance
between us. When the baby let out a burp in my
ear, I chanced turning.

Naomi had her shirt buttoned and Gabriel on
her shoulder, coaxing a burp out of Michael's little
brother. She was grinning at me like we shared a
secret joke, and I rolled my eyes.

"Yeah, I know, it's supposed to be natural," I
said, and she shrugged, letting out a soft laugh.

"I'm sorry if I made you uncomfortable. I just
needed a hand, and since Damian's gone, you were
it." She stood, bringing the baby to one of the empty
bassinets, and changed his diaper and swaddled
him before turning to me with her hands out. "After
yesterday, I don't trust the staff here," she added,
and I relinquished Michael.

I couldn't blame her. I had stayed up all night
because of the same lack of trust.

"Demons suck," I muttered, and she sent a laugh in my direction.

"Yes, they do." She swaddled Michael, putting him in the third bassinet.

"What about Grace?" I looked at the sleeping child.

"She ate a little while ago, before the boys woke." Naomi climbed onto the bed, yawning. "I am so tired."

I helped her with the covers, tucking her in.

"Thank you," she mumbled, and her eyelids dropped.

I thought about going back to my perch outside the door, but I was tired, too, and at least inside the room, I knew there was a barrier between us and hell's minions. I knew if I sat down, I would follow Naomi's lead. That was dangerous, so I stepped next to Grace's crib, staring down at the perfect little angel.

Her eyes blinked open, like she knew she was being observed, and I smiled. A squeak came from her and instead of waking Naomi, I picked up the little bundle, nestling her in my arms, and slowly rocked her.

The child's eyes were a mix of blue and brown swirls that reminded me of my mother's calico eyes and I sighed, crossing to the window as the sadness hit. Grace squealed, kicking at the blanket swaddling her, and I lifted her to my shoulder, cuddling her soft cheek against mine.

"It's okay," I whispered. "Uncle CJ's just a little sad." I rubbed her back, and she cooed once more before letting out a sigh and settling down with her head nestled against my neck. Her warmth wrapped around me, penetrating layers of despair and a flicker of hope lit in my soul.

I would gladly wipe hell off the map for the little
trinity angel in my arms.

Chapter 6

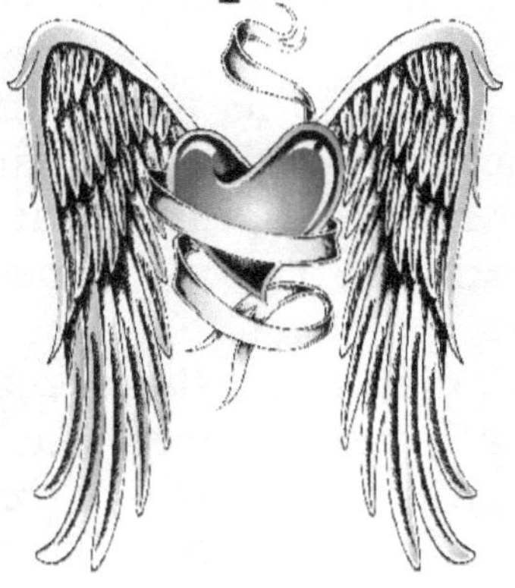

I DON'T KNOW HOW long I stood at the window rocking Grace, but I finally relinquished her to the crib and went back to my post outside the room while Naomi and the babies took a much-needed rest.

A cop wandered by, and I cleared my throat, capturing his attention.

"Did you ever find that cat?" I asked when he stopped in front of the spot of my vigilant watch.

"No." He glanced down the hall toward the operating rooms. "We turned this place upside down, too."

"How do you lose a tiger?" I stretched, rolling my neck to get the kinks out.

The cop chuckled. "I'm beginning to think the guys were pulling my leg." He scratched the back of his scalp and met my gaze. "You know, like an asinine initiation or something." He glanced around and then met my gaze. "The only reason I'm still looking is because a couple of nurses are missing," he whispered.

I swallowed and tried on what I hoped was a shocked expression. "Wouldn't there be some kind of mess if..."

"You would think," he said and straightened. "Watch your back," he added and walked away.

I stared after him and guilt bit at the heels of my conscience. I killed one of those nurses, and Damian killed the other. Of course, they were possessed by demons, so there really wasn't any way around it, at least not one that I was aware of, and none in Damian's history. From what I could glean from his memories, being possessed usually meant the host was dead or had given themselves willingly over to the darkness. They couldn't just take control of a soul at will, which was a good thing in retrospect. Otherwise, I would be Satan's puppet right now.

The elevator dinged, and Damian stepped out with a travel bag slung over his shoulder. I glanced at my watch. It took him three hours to get a car and car seats and he bypassed the room, heading straight to the desk announcing he wanted to have his wife and children released. There really was no leeway in his tone, and the nurse tapped the keyboard.

"What's your wife's name?" she asked.

"Naomi Andreas."

Her fingers flew on the keyboard again. "A-n-d-r-e-a-s?" she asked, spelling the name out, and the muscles in Damian's jaw jumped. He nodded, but I could tell he was getting frustrated.

"I don't have her in the computer," she said, looking up at him.

He pulled up his sleeve and shoved his wrist in her face. "Check again," he said, and I stood, crossing to the desk to intervene.

"She's in the room over there with triplets. I think you were just waiting until they could get a car that held three approved car seats."

She glanced at me offering a smile of thanks and then looked at Damian. "Our records show she was already released. With all the excitement around here, I guess things got a little out of sync." She stood and came around the desk. "I'll do one last verification of your identification tags and then I'll make sure you have enough formula and diapers to hold you over until you can get to a store."

Damian relaxed and gave a nod. "Thank you," he said to her and sent a nod in my direction. The silent thank you resounded in my head as well.

"I'll also need to check the vehicle before you leave," she said as she pushed Naomi's door open.

Damian fished into his pocket, pulling out three tabs and handing them to her. "These were the car seats I ended up getting. They were on your approved list," he said.

She glanced at the make and model on the tag and smiled, nodding and handing them back.

Naomi stepped out of the bathroom, still wearing her hospital gown. The moment her eyes landed on Damian, the tension in her features relaxed. "Home?" she asked, and he nodded even though I knew they didn't have a home right now.

Damian glanced back at me and shrugged. "We're staying with you for a couple of days."

"Really," I said with a laugh, and the seriousness in his gaze shut me up.

The nurse matched up bracelets and checked off items on the clipboard in her hand. Damian put the bag on the bed and began pulling out essentials, like clothing for Naomi and little winter jackets for each of the children. When all was said and done, they had three diaper bags from the hospital stocked with formula and diapers and the travel bag Damian brought.

Naomi dressed, and when she stepped out of the bathroom, I stared at her. If I hadn't witnessed it, I would swear there was no way in hell she had triplets three days ago. I guess transitioning to the tiger really did something incredible to her metabolism.

The nurse stared with the same level of shock and then she flipped through the chart again like something was wrong and her brow wrinkled. "Can I see that wrist band again?"

Naomi held her wrist out again with a smile.

The nurse's eyebrows arched, and she sighed. "I'll be right back with a wheelchair," she said, and when Naomi opened her mouth to argue, the nurse held up her hand. "Hospital policy."

The moment the nurse left, I let out a laugh. "You really don't look like you gave birth to even one child, never mind three." Damian turned toward me. "She doesn't." I shoved my hands in my pocket and glanced out the window, ignoring his probing stare.

His insecurity flared again, and I sighed, sending a look of disdain in his direction. The jackass needed to be a little more confident in how his wife felt about him. He caught my thoughts and irritation flashed in his eyes before he looked away.

"Chill, I'm not making a move on your wife." Although the thought of having a turn at her breasts wasn't something I'd turn down. I just knew the offer would never be extended, at least not while Damian was alive.

He grabbed one bag and threw it in my direction; the glare accompanying the toss meant he got a whiff of my thoughts. I caught the bag and slung it over my shoulder. "Which child do you want me to carry?"

"Why don't you carry Michael," Naomi said, scooping up Grace in her arms.

I stepped to the crib tagged with Michael's name and scooped him up, bringing him to the bed where a winter snuggly was laid out for each child. I slid Michael into the green one. Damian took care of zipping Gabriel into a blue snuggly, leaving the pink one for Grace.

The nurse arrived and our merry little band exited the hospital. After all three kids were hooked into the middle row, I slid into the far back, and leaned back, closing my eyes for the hour-long ride home.

Chapter 7

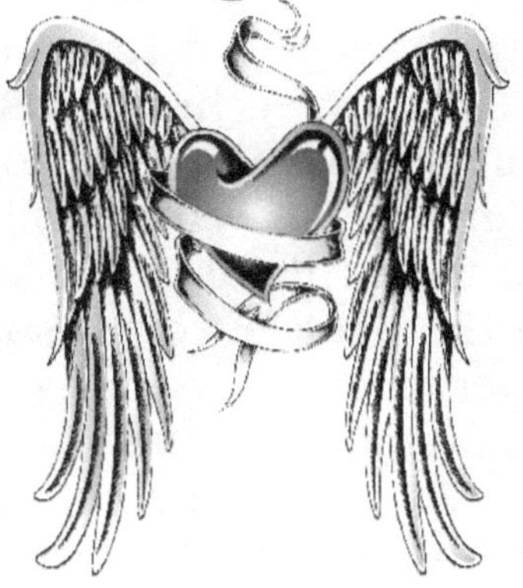

"CHRIS!"

I sat up in the backseat and stared at the figure standing over me. Damian shifted and pulled the last baby seat from the base.

"We're home." He disappeared out the side of the van.

I rubbed my eyes and stepped out, welcoming the salty tinge in the air. Naomi had already gone into the house and Damian slipped inside as I closed the car door. The gates were clear of lurking media, and I was glad they had deserted their posts. I didn't want to deal with that type of irritation, not with the foul mood brewing under my skin.

The minute I stepped into the house, the level of noise fanned those flames and I gave a nod to everyone in the family room. My gaze lingered on my brother's and even without the benefit of mind reading, I knew he wasn't handling our father's death well. I sent him a nod and escaped into the basement, to our workout area. Specifically, to the punching bag.

I stripped my jacket, tossing it into the corner, and approached the bag, allowing the turmoil inside to curl my hands into fists. The first jab felt good, the scrape of the leather across my knuckles, the slight give of the bag, the rattle of the chains, all fueled me, and my jabs became full punches, each one more brutal than the last.

Scenes from the past few days snapped off in my mind, each punctuated by my fists connecting with the leather. The faster the mind show, the faster my fists flew, and the more my fury bloomed. My breath labored and I finally let out a warrior cry and slammed my right fist in the center of the target with everything I had. The bag flew across the basement, smashing into the far wall, disintegrating into a puff of Styrofoam.

I stared at the mess and then my gaze dropped to my hands, still clenched at the ready. Blood flowed from my knuckles, and I loosened my fists, wincing at the first sign of pain now that I wasn't numb with anger.

"Ah, fuck." I turned toward the stairs and stopped.

"Finished?" Tom signed from his position at the bottom of the stairs.

"What do you think?" I snapped, dropping my throbbing hands to my side. Warm trails of blood dribbled down my fingers, the sensation distracting and calming at the same time.

"I think you're just gearing up," he signed and cocked an eyebrow. "Want to tell me what happened?"

The air went out of my chest, and I shook my head. I didn't want to talk about Sandy, and I sure as hell didn't want to talk about fucking a demon.

"Are you okay?"

I let a bark of a laugh loose. Am I okay? Well, that was the fifty-thousand-dollar question, and I shrugged. "Are you?"

He looked beyond me at what was left of the punching bag and shook his head. When his eyes found mine, they glistened with an unshed layer of tears.

My laughter faded, and I took a closer look, not just at his physical appearance, but at his mind as well. The severed head of my father brought back the nightmare he endured in Georgia, and I crossed, pulling him into a hug. The kid deserved better than what he had been dealt and while he had shut me out at that time of his life; I was the one who he turned to this time.

"I'm sorry I took off," I said when the shakes started, I wasn't sure if it was Tom or me who was trembling, but he was the one crying and holding on like I was the only thing keeping his sanity in check.

Fear radiated from him and without words, I got the litany of nightmares that plagued him these last few nights. Nightmares that he carried alone. Not even Steve had been privy to his sweat-induced terror. Past and present had blended into a carnival of blades and blood, wreaking havoc on everyone he loved.

He couldn't articulate to Raven, not in any way that communicated the depth of the horrors he faced. It had been years since Georgia haunted him and now it was as if the killer had risen in his nightmares, taking vengeance on him for surviving.

"That's not the first time Dad lost his head," I said when the shakes stopped.

Tom pushed me away, his damp face cracking a smile. "You're sick," he signed and then mopped his face with his sleeve.

I grinned and looked at the floor. "Yeah, well, sometimes all you need is a well-placed joke." I glanced up at him.

"Thank you," he signed. "Now that I've unloaded, think you want to tell me what happened with Sandy?"

My smile disappeared, and I looked at the destroyed punching bag instead of my brother. "She found someone else." I grabbed the broom from the closet under the stairs. I crossed and started sweeping the miniature Styrofoam balls into a neat little pile.

When I looked up, Tom wasn't there anymore, but my flash of irritation was short-lived. He trotted down the stairs with the box of garbage bags and another broom. He quietly helped me clean up my mess.

We had the foam cleaned up in no time and I leaned on the broom, staring at the group of full garbage bags, and it occurred to me he had only been dumped once. That travesty had led him to Raven.

"Damian told me everything happens for a reason."

Tom glanced up from tying the last bag. He bit his lip and sighed before his hands slowly signed. "I used to think that was bullshit," he started, and I could hear the words forming in his head as he signed. "But since I met Raven, I'm not so sure it is." He shrugged and shoved his hands in his pocket, signaling he had nothing to add for the moment.

His answer surprised me, considering the shit he's been through. "So, you really think everything is predetermined?"

He shrugged and picked up a couple of bags, waiting for me to follow suit. I grabbed the remaining garbage and headed upstairs, holding the door for him. The murmuring in the kitchen stopped the moment we appeared. All eyes followed us through the house and into the garage and when I stepped back inside, behind Tom, Jennifer crossed her arms, raising her eyebrow at me.

I glanced at my bloody knuckles and then back at her with a shrug. "I'll live," I said to her silent scrutiny and crossed to the kitchen sink, turning on the cold water. I glanced at the reflections in the window and sent a warning glare as Steve stepped closer.

"Leave it." Stinging pain bit at my knuckles as the water washed away the blood, numbing all other sensations floating through me. I pressed my teeth together, not quite clenching, more like grinding them slowly until the water ran clear. After turning the faucet off, I wrapped a sheet of paper towel over each hand, gripping the ends to keep it in place before glancing at Steve and Jennifer. "My knuckles are only skinned, not broken," I said to Steve. "If they're bothering me tomorrow, I'll let you do your magic."

"Fine," he replied, raising his hands and stepping away.

"If you're going to be a stubborn jackass, at least let me bandage them properly," Jennifer said, grabbing the rarely used first aid kit from under the sink.

I had little choice in the matter. She grabbed my arm and led me to the table, pointing at the chair. Jennifer peeled the paper towel away, wincing at the raw skin, and I glanced beyond Tom at the empty family room.

"Where's Damian and the rest of the gang?"

"They're upstairs. Raven's helping them get settled for the night. I guess they'll be looking for a house tomorrow," Jennifer said, dabbing some antibiotic ointment on my wounds.

The cool sensation soothed the sting and buffered the cuts from the scrape of the gauze she wrapped around my knuckles. When she finished, she looked at the patch job and nodded, pushing back her seat and giving me a quick pat on the shoulder.

"That should prevent you from bleeding all over the furniture."

"Thanks," I mumbled. My phone buzzed. I dug it out of my pocket and laughed at the name on the display, turning it towards Tom. "Do you remember Jenna?"

His eyebrows rose, and he grinned, nodding and meeting my gaze. She was one of the many girls he screwed around with in high school, and his grin told me what I wanted to know.

"Why is she texting you?" he signed.

"I changed my relationship status on Facebook last night." I scrolled through the messages on my social networking page for the first time since I changed it. I chuckled at the sheer number of 'call me' messages and then I brought up Jenna's personal invitation.

"Looks like she's having a party," I said, and met Tom's gaze again.

Tom glanced at Steve and then signed, "I remember her parties being pretty wild."

I could use a little wild right now, especially wild with a non-possessed woman. I typed out a response and moments later, her address appeared on my screen. I knew the area, and I gave Tom a nod. "I'm going out for a bit," I said to Steve and Jennifer and didn't wait for them to intercede. I was out of the house and on the road in a matter of minutes.

Chapter 8

I GLANCED AT THE house and then the address on my phone. It matched, but the house wasn't overrun with people like the few high school parties that we used to crash. Of course, Jenna wasn't in high school anymore, and I crossed to the door, pocketing my phone. I hesitated. The absence of thought raised flags, and I pulled my hand away from the doorbell.

I was no longer sure this was a good idea, but then the door swung open and there Jenna Sylvan stood. In high school, she was one of the prettiest girls, and she had turned into a smoking hot woman. I stared at the skimpy negligee she wore. Stunned into silence, I didn't move. She reached out, grabbed my coat, and yanked me inside.

The door closed and smokey air filtered through the house. I sniffed and found my voice. "Getting high?" I asked as she stripped my coat.

"Among other things." She tossed my coat on the railing, leading me into the living room.

I stopped in the entryway. The coffee table was littered with all manner of drugs, from joints to pills to neatly cut lines of coke, and Jenna wasn't alone. Being a cop's son, I had steered clear of drugs for the most part. I've only experienced a hit of marijuana twice, and nothing like the spread before me. And Jenna wasn't alone. Two former cheerleaders looked up from their position on the floor. Both of them were naked and one was snorting lines off the other's stomach. I don't know whether or not it was a blessing, but I couldn't recall their names.

"Welcome to the party," they giggled, and I glanced at Jenna wondering if Tom knew she swung both ways.

"Don't look so shocked," she said, coaxing me forward and into the lone chair. She handed me a lit joint, and I looked at it, debating. "We have dreamed of having you alone, all to ourselves, for as long as I can remember."

I stared at her stoned eyes and brought the joint to my lips, inhaling a deep pull and holding it, despite the overriding need to cough. "How long have you been doing that shit?" I squeaked out and exhaled, pointing my chin toward the table.

"A few years." Her hands traveled to my belt. I took another hit and reached down, stilling her busy fingers.

"I don't have anything," I said. I hadn't come prepared, and all I needed was to knock up the town slut.

She laughed at me and turned, reaching beyond the drugs to a small bowl, and pulled a strip of condoms from inside, holding them up for me. "We thought that might be the case. You were always so straight-laced in high school. Unlike your brother," she whispered, and I laughed, staring at the package and letting my gaze travel to the two girls exploring each other.

"Damn," I whispered and took a third hit, sucking as the burning embers glowed.

Jenna's eyes focused on the bandages on my knuckles and her hands left my unbuckled belt, choosing to trace the bandages instead. Her gray eyes looked up at me, filled with concern. "You're hurt."

"Nah, just scraped the crap out of my hands. I'll be fine." The pot had started to weed its way into my bloodstream like a numbing agent, and I handed her back the joint. She put it on the table and pulled me to her lips. Her kiss was empty and did nothing to get my engine revved, but when she unbuttoned my shirt and lick her way from my neck to my waistband, I didn't stop her.

She chuckled, and I let her pull my jeans off and accepted the offer of another joint. I smoked the entire thing while the girls took turns blowing me. I had never been this high, this fast, each hit taking me farther into the land of sensations and sex.

"What the hell is this?" I asked, inspecting the stub of a joint between my fingers. Jenna looked up from my lap with a wicked grin.

"Maui laced with a little of everything," she whispered and took me in her mouth again.

I closed my eyes and let them take me to the land of excess.

"OH, FUCK." BRIGHT RAYS of sunshine blinded me. I attempted to roll away, but I was blocked in by bodies draped over me. My head pounded and every muscle in my body ached. Bleached blonde hair covered my chest and I wasn't sure whose head it belonged to.

I blinked, squinting at the ceiling, and the events of the night bled into my memory. I pushed the bodies off and sat up, scanning the family room and the remnants of drugs strewn about, along with the number of used condoms. I think I used up their entire stockpile. Holy shit.

Jenna stirred next to me, her sleepy eyes focused on me for a moment and then her eyelids dropped again, and I hopped to my feet, finding each piece of clothing and pulling it on. For the second time in as many nights, I did the walk of shame, but actually this time, I didn't slink from the place like at the hospital; instead, I stumbled out the door to my car, tumbled into the driver's seat, and fumbled for my keys. My stomach did a slow roll, and I clenched my teeth against the acid burn in my throat, focusing on getting the hell out of there.

Tom had been right. Jenna was kinky as hell and her friends had matched her carnal appetite, leaving me at the mercy of three very stoned, very horny women. I drank it in like a man who had been lost in the desert for days and just stumbled upon an oasis, but during the night, I heard the devil's whisper, promising this type of decadence for the rest of my days if I'd just allow him in.

I swerved to the side of the road and swung the door open, just in time for whatever was in my stomach to purge all over the pavement.

Had I? Jesus, did I say yes?

I shivered, closing my eyes and willing the details out of the fog. What I saw left me shaking with relief, but the shit thing was, I'd considered it. When the devil offered the option of Naomi to me in the same compromising positions as Jenna, I actually considered his fucked-up offer.

I stared out the window, wondering if he had offered Sandy instead of Naomi, would I have said yes?

Chapter 9

THE HOUSE WAS QUIET, and I glanced at the clock. It was a little after three in the afternoon. I fished out my phone and stared at the home screen. No missed calls. Well, at least they hadn't started a search party. Instead of heading toward the back of the house where Steve and Jennifer's home office was, to see if they were there, I climbed the stairs, heading to the bathroom to clean up. The mint freshness of the toothpaste felt good in my sour mouth, and I stared at my bloodshot eyes. Disappointment raked across my skin, and I dropped my gaze. I didn't want to psychoanalyze my behavior.

I knew I went too far.

The warm water of the shower washed away the dried evidence of a wild night and I stood under the spray, contemplating Steve's reaction to my lapse of judgment. I knew Steve was going to be pissed when he found out I got wasted. I just hoped he wouldn't get a glimpse of my drug induced sexcapades. I shut off the water and wrapped a towel around my waist. I didn't think twice about stepping out of the bathroom in only a towel, but when the door opened and Naomi's surprised gaze met mine, I halted.

"Where is everyone?" she asked.

I shrugged and smiled at the way her eyes bounced from mine to my bare chest.

"What the hell happened to you?"

My smile faded, and I looked at my bare chest for the first time since I left Jenna's. Deep welts crisscrossed my skin, like the girls had raked their nails across me in the heat of our sexual tryst, but the thing that drew breath from my lungs was the five puncture wounds surrounding my heart, just deep enough to penetrate skin, but not deep enough to do lasting damage. It was like someone, or something, had tried to rip out my heart.

Icy terror layered over me, and I snapped my gaze to hers while I reached for the door to steady myself. I didn't realize just how close the devil's bid for my soul had come to succeeding.

"I... uh," I didn't know what to say, and she shifted the baby on her shoulder.

"Who did this to you?" Concern filled her features, causing Grace to let out a wail. Naomi reached for me, her fingers tracing the bloodless welts before her gaze met mine again. "Lucifer?" she asked in a hushed voice.

"I honestly don't know," I said. I had no memory of anything but mind-altering drugs and kinked-out sex. Lucifer's offer surfaced, the seductive whisper, my consideration, the pain... and everything snapped into place.

My eyes widened and my grip on the doorframe tightened.

In a manner of speaking, I had come so close to being royally fucked. The thought produced a high-pitched laugh, and I ran my hand through my hair.

Sidestepping Naomi, I headed to my bedroom, closing the door on the questions in her eyes.

No wonder everything hurt. Those girls were possessed by more than just drugs, and the things they did brought me to my knees. Before they turned the tables on me, I ravished the depths of their pussies, their asses, and their mouths, coming more times than humanly possible.

I vaguely remember lounging in the chair, while Jenna sprinkled what I thought was coke in my lap. She put a light layer on her breast and pulled my mouth toward her. The white powder numbed my mouth and brought me back to relative consciousness before sending me into orbit.

They had an array of toys and while I seemed to float in and out of awareness; they played with their toys, pleasuring each other until their moans drenched me. I recall drinking from something they handed me and then whispers filled my world, warning me, telling me to wake up, but I ignored them, letting the numb pleasure take over.

I woke at one point with my wrists tied behind my back and the rope nearly strangling me. Jenna had my ear between her teeth and her hand around my cock while her friend sucked and sucked like I had the secret to immortality hidden in my dick.

My drug induced haze cleared when her hips pressed against my backside, and I realized I was the benefactor of one of her toys. I struggled, choking on the pressure from the bindings, my body tingling back to life from her vigorous thrusts. There was no pain, and a different level of ecstasy gripped me. Jenna's grunts mixed with the others and my entire body seized, my orgasm flooding the mouth of the sucking queen.

Jenna's hands ripped across my chest, drawing the crisscross pattern Naomi saw and she didn't slow her pace. The ominous whisper in my ear, along with the pain in my chest, brought me to another brink; a brink filled with empty promises as her nails slid into my flesh.

How I wanted to say yes, the idea of ravishing Naomi, taking her any way I damned well pleased was so appealing, even though I knew how wrong it all was. I was so close to giving in when another mouth latched onto my hardening member, sucking me into submission.

My father's voice filled my head with a warning that overshadowed everything else, and the rope holding me hostage snapped.

I had the wherewithal to yank her hand from my chest and buck her off before the word "no" slipped from my lips. Jenna's cheeks flushed in anger and then her friend pushed me against the wall, resuming the task of swallowing every inch of me. My eyes rolled back with the next wave.

I remembered nothing after that.

I sat down on my bed, aroused at the memories and disgusted with myself for being such a fucking freak. Demons sure knew how to take advantage of a guy when he's down.

My bedroom door opened, and Tom stared at me, his eyes widening at the raw scrapes crossing my chest.

"Why didn't you tell me she was a drug-crazed bitch in heat?" I asked. I couldn't help the flare of anger that surfaced, and he closed the door behind him.

"Drugs?" he signed and cocked his head.

"Yes. She was a regular fucking drug store." I pulled my pants on, zipping them up before meeting his gaze.

"Like what?"

"Pot. Coke. She had pills, too, but I have no idea what they were." I stared at him and then dropped my gaze. "Hell, they could have been roofies for all I know," I added and opened the bureau, pulling out a sweater and slipping it over my head. "And she wasn't alone."

Tom's lips stretched into a grin that just fueled my anger.

"Did you know she has toys, too?"

His eyebrow shot up in the silent question and I saw a little of his memories as he thought about his experience with Jenna. It was eons tamer than what I experienced, without a toy in sight.

I laughed.

"Compared to last night, your roll in the hay with her was nothing more than a boring workout," I said, and his mouth popped open into a small 'o' of surprise. "Yeah, imagine three girls and every conceivable position you can think of, and then add a half a dozen more that you've never dreamed of," I said, and he grinned. "It's not grin worthy, Tom. Fucking three girls while in a drug-induced haze isn't something to pat me on the back for."

His smile dropped. "You got wasted?"

"Out of my goddamned mind." I ran the brush through my wet hair, slicking it back before turning and facing my brother. "And I'm not sure it was Jenna."

His brow scrunched. "What do you mean?"

"I think she and her friends were possessed by more than just the drugs." I looked out the window at the ocean. "Maybe I was, too, for a bit." When I turned back in his direction, his arms crossed and he waited for more of an explanation.

"It seems the devil wants my soul."

Tom shrugged. "The devil wants everyone's soul," he signed.

I couldn't argue with him there, but he didn't understand exactly why Lucifer was targeting me. "He wants me because I can destroy Damian and deliver Naomi and Grace to the twisted fuck."

Tom's arms slowly unfolded, and his eyes widened as the scope of the devil's tricks unfolded in his mind.

"And the bastard somehow knows I've got the hots for Naomi," I admitted, and Tom laughed.

"She is beautiful," he signed, and his cheeks turned red.

It made me feel marginally better that my brother had the same attraction to the woman. "Yeah, but she's in love with Damian, all the way down to the cellular level, like Mom was with Dad." I leaned against the bed. "Unfortunately, Lucifer knows I'm... vulnerable right now, and he is playing with me."

"How?"

"He's throwing some serious instruments of seduction at me." I met his gaze and saw the confusion in his eyes. Before he could ask, I continued, "There was a nurse at the hospital. I was exhausted, and she showed me to the nurse's lounge."

"What happened?"

I looked up at him. "She was hot." I couldn't help the smile that played on my lips. "After we screwed around, she tried to persuade me to let Lucifer in, just like Jenna did last night. Unfortunately, the nurse had the gall to reveal the demon inside her and I annihilated the bitch."

"Annihilated?"

"Turned her to dust," I said and snapped my fingers. "Gone, dead, whatever."

"You killed a nurse?"

"I killed a demon," I corrected.

He dropped his gaze. His mind jumped to Jenna and his eyes snapped back to mine.

"No, I didn't kill Jenna," I answered the unspoken question. "I probably should have, but I was too far gone. Hell, between the drugs and the mind-blowing sex, I almost said yes to her." I met his gaze. "I think Dad somehow got a warning through to me."

Shock transformed his face. "But..."

"Yeah, I know, he's gone, locked behind the pearly gates with the rest of the fallen angels, but I swear he got a message through to me."

"What did he say?"

I chuckled. "He told me to get my shit together."

Tom smiled. "Sounds like something Dad would say," he signed.

"Yeah." I had nothing else to add to the conversation, so I just shrugged and dug my hands into my pockets, wincing at the scrape of my knuckles on the fabric. I looked at the floor. "Do me a favor?" I asked, without looking up at him.

"Sure?" his voice echoed in my head, and I met his gaze.

"If I fuck up, I want you to be the one to take me out."

His complexion paled, and he shook his head.

"You'd be the only one I'd let close enough, Tom. You're family, and if I screw up for some ungodly reason, you've got to kill me. Otherwise..." My gaze dropped to the ground. I didn't want to entertain what would happen if the devil got his way.

"No." His perfect enunciation pulled my gaze to him. Tom crossed the room and grabbed a fistful of my shirt, pulling me close to his furious features. "You will not screw up." His words came from his mind, not his tightly clamped mouth, and they

came with the power of a hurricane, ringing in my
ears as his eyes leveled the challenge.

Chapter 10

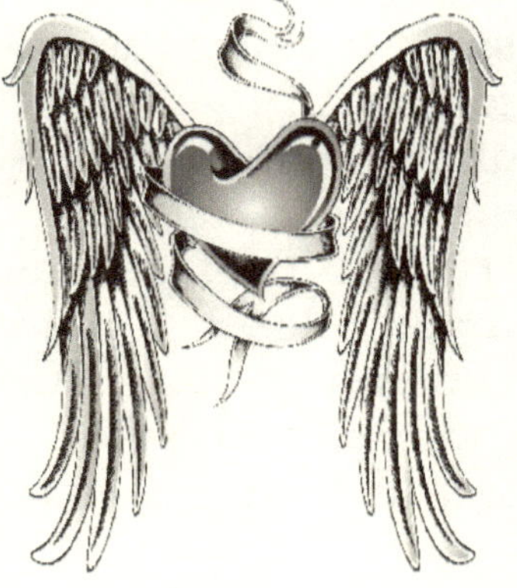

I ROLLED ONTO MY side and blinked my eyes open. Noise drifted from downstairs, a mixture of babies crying, and people talking, and I stretched, squeezing my eyes closed against the sharp pain behind them. Eventually, I slid out of bed and headed to the bathroom in search of aspirin to take the edge off my headache.

Moving my hands resulted in flares of pain as well, and I leaned my forehead against the pantry door, breathing for a moment before continuing. Opening the bottle presented a challenge, and I was too damned tired to will the thing open, so I headed downstairs.

Conversation stopped when I stepped into the room and held the aspirin up. "Can someone open this for me?" Even my voice sounded haggard and raw.

It was Steve who crossed the space, ripping the bottle from my grip. His angry glare penetrated every fiber and I think I flinched. I know I took a step back.

"I understand you decided, in your infinite wisdom, that drugs were the answer to your problems," he said, shaking the bottle at me like a weird exclamation point.

My gaze bounced from him to Tom beyond and back.

"Tom didn't rat you out," he said, clenching his teeth, and he stepped closer. "Banging everything in a skirt isn't the answer, either." This time there was less bite to his words, and I met his gaze. He had been there before. In both places, and I gave him a sheepish nod.

"I didn't..." I started and studied the patterns in the carpet at my feet. "I didn't intend to get wasted." I forced myself to meet his gaze.

Steve could be intimidating when he wanted, and he knew how to push the guilt buttons. I had to give him a great deal of credit for taking us in and raising us like we were his own, and I hated like hell to disappoint the man. But that's exactly what I saw in his eyes. Disappointment. And it made me feel like I was ten years old again.

"Can you just open the aspirin?" I whispered, hating the pathetic lilt in my voice.

"I should just let you suffer," he muttered, and his lips pressed together. Instead of opening the container, he pulled my forehead to his lips, opting to give me one more dose of excruciating pain before the tingling started in my hands, my chest, and behind my eyes.

"Damn it, I didn't ask you to fix it. I asked you to open the fucking aspirin." I stepped back, grabbing the stair railing to steady the after-shakes of his healing power.

"Next time, I'll beat the shit out of you." He pointed and turned away, leaving me huffing against the wall.

Silence blanketed the room, and I slid to a seat on the steps, cradling my head while Steve's power magically erased the pain. After a few seconds, the crew resumed their conversations, and I glanced between my splayed fingers.

Only one person focused on me, his glare sharp over the edge of his laptop, and I dropped my gaze, avoiding Damian's silent rage. I stood, unsure of where to go to get away from the commotion and his justified anger. I had nearly sold his family out, and instead of confronting it head on, I slipped out the back door and took a seat on one of the lounge chairs, letting the cold wind saturate my clothing.

The door opened, and I stiffened, meeting his gaze as he took the seat next to me and handed me a beer. He didn't speak at first, just stared out at the open ocean, and drained half the bottle.

"I get it," he said after a while.

"You get what?"

"Naomi. I get why you might be tempted to trade your soul for her."

I sighed. "No offense, but I really wouldn't trade my soul for her." I took a sip of beer. "There just isn't that 'I gotta have her' connection." I met his gaze. "I was high and horny, and I guess getting a viewing of her chest the other day at the hospital put some unsavory thoughts in my head." I shrugged.

Damian chugged the rest of his beer, the knuckles on his hand gripping the bottle turning white as he squeezed the glass. "You what?" he asked, planting the bottle on the cold concrete.

"She needed help breast feeding the boys while you were out getting a car." I tried not to smirk, but it appeared anyway.

His face turned red, and his hands clenched.

"Look, I told you the first night you were here, I wasn't interested in making a play for her," I said. "I'm still not."

He took a deep breath, calming the coil inside, and I waited, gearing myself up for an attack. Damian surprised me by getting up and crossing to the rock wall, where he swung a leg over the wall and took a seat. He stared out at the Nubble Lighthouse in the distance, blocking me from the thoughts going through his mind.

His expression told me nothing, and I waited and wondered how much of my sordid evening he got wind of. His head turned toward me and the muscles in his jaw jumped.

"You made the mistake of leaving them alive," he said, too quietly to carry over the distance, but his voice was loud and clear in my head.

His penetrating glare painted a picture in my mind, and I shot to my feet, approaching him. "What did you do?"

He stared me down and then looked out at the ocean.

"Damian," I snapped, even though I had a clear idea.

"I took care of it," he said.

"You killed them?" A shiver spread through me and then I thought about the DNA evidence strewn all over the family room. Evidence that would point to me.

"It's all gone. The demons, the drugs, the fucking house. It's just a pile of dust and burning embers."

"I'm not sure they were all possessed," I balked. "Jenna, sure, but her friends, I didn't know, and I couldn't take the chance of killing innocents."

"And I couldn't take the chance they weren't."

I stared at him, popping my mouth closed. His cavalier attitude toward killing reminded me of my father. He was a master at justifying it, too. "What gives you the right?"

He swung his leg back and stood, crowding me. "Twenty-five hundred years of dealing with demons. Knowing how they operate, how they manipulate their victims. If I'd let them live, they would have ditched the meat suits and gone onto someone else. Maybe someone you wouldn't have had the ability to say no to." He stepped closer, his gaze hard and unyielding. "And you would have been implicated in whatever they left behind."

I gave him some space and shoved my clenched hands into my pockets.

"If they can't get you to say yes, they ruin your life to the point you don't give a damn. Either way, they win." He stopped and took a deep breath. "I was not only protecting my wife and kids, but I was also protecting your ass, too."

I kicked a patch of frozen grass and scanned the cold ocean. I didn't like what he did, but it was no different from what I did to the nurse, and I eventually nodded. "Are you sure there isn't a way to exorcise a demon?" I needed to know if there was a way we could save the souls they pillaged.

"Without killing the host?" Damian sighed and shook his head. "No."

I took a moment to scrutinize his memories. What I came back with was confirmation, and I turned back toward the house, trudging across the lawn, and sat back in the lounge chair. The chill in the air had been replaced with a chill in my soul, and a dark fear encompassed me.

What if they ever got a hold of Sandy?

Chapter 11

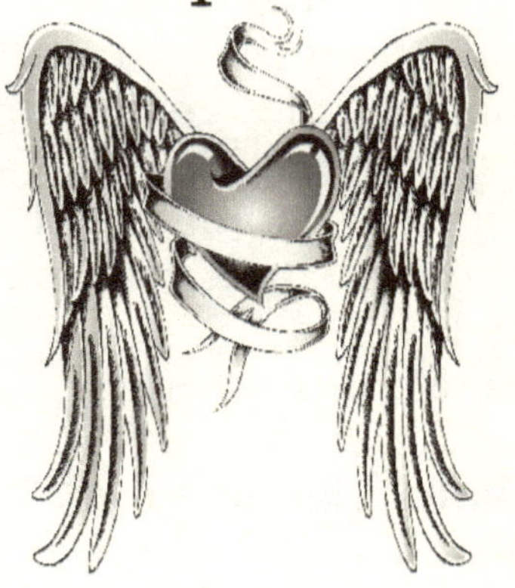

“DID YOU FIND A house?” Jennifer asked when everyone was settled at the dinner table. She passed the rolls and focused on Damian.

“Yes,” Damian said, digging into a pile of pasta on his plate. “It’s actually just down the road. I negotiated a move in date on the first of next month.” He glanced across the table at Steve. “In the meantime, we’ll grab a hotel room after tonight.”

“You are welcome to stay here until the closing,” Jennifer said, rocking Grace in her arms. The two boys were sound asleep in new strollers near the table.

I exchanged a glance with Tom. Our nice quiet home had become a mini-day care, and I took a bite of the spaghetti. He gave me that ‘it isn’t that bad’ look and slid his gaze to Raven. She was enamored with the babies as much as Jennifer was.

Damian opened his mouth to answer, and his cell phone rang, interrupting the conversation. He looked at the display and said, “Excuse me,” before taking the call. Damian’s face paled as he held the phone to his ear and his gaze traveled to mine. The panic written in his irises gave me pause and I closed my eyes, pulling the gist of the conversation from his fragmented thoughts. I opened my eyes when he ended the call.

"What's going on?" Naomi asked, pulling him out of his broken thoughts and reading the concern in his face accurately.

"Ted says there's a problem at the hospital." His voice cracked.

"Is Valerie okay?" Naomi asked.

Damian laughed and looked at the ceiling, his eyes glazing over in a way I hadn't seen.

I took a moment to scan his memories for the name Valerie and came up with a wealth of information. He had known Valerie from the day she was born and considered her the closest thing he had to family. He felt responsible for letting a demon get to her, and her uncle Ted shared that feeling, asking Damian to leave their home after the attack on his niece nearly took her life.

I equated the kinship Damian felt with Valerie with what Steve and Jennifer felt for us and instinctively knew he would have never left her if he thought she was in danger. Both he and her Uncle Ted thought being safely tucked away in Hartford Hospital would keep her away from Lucifer's greedy grip.

Damian blinked his eyes clear and focused back on his wife. "For now, but Ted has a feeling come nightfall they'll send something that can breach the salt line.

Naomi looked at the fading sun outside the family room windows, blanching the way Damian had. She didn't need to say what the fearful look in her eyes meant, and Damian didn't either, but one word resounded in both their heads. Vampires.

"Is he armed?" she asked.

Damian shook his head. "I have to get there as fast as I can."

He glanced at me, and I knew that his chosen mode of transportation involved nothing that encased him in metal. His fastest bet was taking on the hawk form and from his expression, he didn't know if he could pull that off.

His gaze moved to Steve, and he looked at the phone in his hand, zeroing in on the man's unique gift set. "Can you really do that two places at once, shit?"

Steve traded a glance with Tom and Raven before meeting Damian's gaze. "Yes."

"Can you do that and still wipe out anything that tries to hurt them?"

Steve slid his gaze to Jennifer and nodded. "Yeah, I can still smoke a demon," he said to Damian's worried train of thought.

"Can you stay with them until I get there?"

This time, Steve hesitated and put his fork down. "I don't know if I'll be able to hold the connection for that long." It wasn't so much what he said, but the underlying fear that if he left his own family unprotected, bad things might happen.

"We can make sure the house here is protected," I said. "Besides, I have a feeling Damian will get there within an hour."

Steve silently debated, and some of it filtered through to me. When he met my gaze, I shrugged a shoulder, giving him a what-the-hell gaze. He drew a deep breath, his chest expanding before he blew a stream of air through his lips. He turned to Damian and gave a quick nod before wiping his mouth with a napkin. He excused himself from the kitchen table and crossed to the new leather recliner, and settled in before meeting Damian's gaze.

"I need a connection. Do you mind calling your friend back and leaving your phone here with me?"

Damian fumbled with the phone, and I covered a smirk with my hand, trading glances with Tom and Jennifer. They wore the same amused smile I was covering. Damian glared at us and then held the phone to his ear.

"Ted, I've got some help coming. He's one of the good guys," he said and held the phone out for Steve.

"Hi, Ted. My name is Steve, and I need you to take a seat and keep the phone line open no matter what, okay?"

After a moment, all the animation left Steve. Damian stared at Steve's waxy figure sitting stalk-still. After a few stunned blinks, Damian traded a glance with Naomi and his eyebrows rose in a 'get a load of this shit' way that forced a chuckle from my throat.

Their minds both broadcast the word "Freak."

"Oh, come on," I said to Naomi. "You change into a fucking tiger, for God's sake." Then I turned toward Damian. "And you, you're just as much of a freak of nature as he is."

Damian let a huff of a laugh and gave Naomi a quick peck on the forehead. "I'll have Steve give you the phone when I get there," he said before he bolted out the front door.

Naomi waited for a few moments and then met my gaze, her eyebrows scrunching together in a question. "I didn't hear the car."

"Seems Damian still has that hawk gene." I sent a wink in her direction and refocused on my meal.

"You're kidding?"

I shook my head. "He actually gave me a lift to the roof of the hospital the other night when you turned tiger in the nursery. It was a little unsettling.”

“Oh. He didn’t say anything,” she said and stared at her food.

The hurt in her voice took me and everyone else at the table by surprise. I finished the last bite on my plate and wiped my lips with my napkin before I replied. “You two kind of have your hands full,” I said, waving towards the three kids. “I’m not sure he’s had more than a couple of hours of sleep in the last few nights.”

“I’m just as tired as he is,” she said, her voice took on a defensive lilt. Raven put her arm around Naomi’s shoulders and gave her a little squeeze.

“Men,” she whispered and added an eye roll that pulled a ghost of a smile to Naomi’s pouting lips.

I stood and cleared my plate. “I’m not saying you aren’t just as tired. I’m just saying he was a little more concerned with your safety than mentioning his ability had resurfaced.”

She nodded and glanced at Steve. “What do we do with him?”

“Just leave him be,” Jennifer answered and cleared the rest of the empty plates.

I sat down next to the living corpse and turned on the television, flipping through the channels while Jennifer and Raven helped Naomi with the babies. Tom wandered in and took a seat on the other couch.

“I’ll never get used to that,” he signed, and I huffed, glancing at Steve’s waxy complexion.

I’m not sure I’ll ever get used to astral projection, either. It’s one ability I’m glad I don’t have. It’s beyond disconcerting, but it comes in handy at times like these when Steve needs to be in two places at once, especially when there is a lag time between the distress call and when the cavalry rides in.

When my mother used to do this, I could still read her thoughts, but whenever my father or Steve projected, I lost the contact. In other words, I was in the blind. Which is not the most comfortable place to be when I knew he was in danger. I shifted and then decided maybe we should be a little more pragmatic.

"Jen, did you buy salt at the store?" I asked over my shoulder, my gaze traveling to the darkening sky outside.

"I bought half a dozen canisters," she said, and I returned my gaze to hers, picking up the haunting thoughts resounding in her head.

"Mind throwing me one?" I stood and waited, catching the Morton's when she tossed it. Without explanation, I lined the doors and windows, creating a demon buffer for the occupants in the house. I considered getting Steve's gun out of his room along with the platinum rounds, but I didn't think Jennifer would be very keen on that with the infants around. It was one thing to have Steve carrying. He was an expert shot, but as far as we were concerned, she didn't have the same blind faith.

I set the nearly empty container on the counter and shot a smile in their direction before returning to my seat. The salt provided a safety net that made me feel marginally better about getting lost in the television program.

The babies were fed and put down in their infant car seats and Jennifer, Raven, and Naomi settled into the couches with us. The knot between my shoulder blades loosened a fraction with everyone in close proximity. I handed Jennifer the remote and let her drive the entertainment for the evening.

Halfway through the latest sitcom, Steve winced, pulling air between his teeth in a hiss, and our gazes jumped from the television to him. Every muscle was taut and the blood vessels in his neck became a relief map of blue against the pallid skin.

"Oh, shit," Naomi cursed and jumped off the couch, grabbing Steve's exposed forearm. Thin lines of blood flowed from two puncture wounds in the meat of his forearm. Before I understood what she was doing, she ripped her belt off and looped it around his upper arm, tightening the makeshift tourniquet.

I didn't understand all the to-do about the small punctures in his arm until Naomi dropped to her knees and covered them with her mouth and sucked. Without warning, she pulled away and spit a bloody glob on the floor. It reminded me of someone sucking poison from a snake bite, and I shivered.

I tuned Jennifer's panicked questions out, along with the infant wail that filled the room. Instead, I spun and stalked to the bar, reaching over and grabbing the Grey Goose Vodka and returning to Naomi and her suck, spit routine. When she pulled away to spit, I doused his arm with the alcohol, hoping it would kill the vampire poison traveling in his bloodstream.

He didn't reanimate either, which told me more than I wanted to admit. It meant he was still battling whatever was attacking them and it had to have attacked without warning. Otherwise, Steve would have gotten the drop on the bastards.

Steve's waxy pallor turned almost gray, a feat I didn't think possible, and I traded a glance with Tom, praying that my mounting panic wasn't as visible as his. Before I could say anything to appease his fears, Naomi grabbed the bottle from me, taking a swig and spitting it out, diluting the small puddle of blood on the floor.

Raven rocked with Grace in her arms, the baby flailing for her mother and crying like a siren warning of the coming darkness. Jennifer gripped Steve's unmarked hand, the slow progress of tears marring her perfect features.

Naomi wiped her mouth and then put her hand on Jennifer's shoulder and squeezed. Without a word, she stood, crossing into the kitchen to grab paper towels and Clorox Wipes to clean and disinfect the floor.

"He's still alive and bleeding. That's a good sign. From what I understand, the shadow virus kills fast. I think if he was going to die, he would have by now," Naomi said, wrapping the soiled paper into a ball and tossing it into the garbage.

I narrowed my eyes into a glare. She was lying through her teeth, and she flicked her gaze to me and then back to Jennifer, forming a fake smile that Jennifer bought. While relief flooded through Jennifer, my muscles clenched painfully as the thought of Steve suffering a long, slow death stunned me.

My gaze landed on the oozing puncture wounds, and I forced myself to swallow the bile lining my throat. I reached and pulled the phone from his hand, listening to the chaos on the other line. Glass crashed, and Damian's snarl echoed through the room.

And then silence blanketed the phone line.

"Fuck," Steve muttered and pulled his arm to his chest, curling over in the seat, resting his forehead on his knees.

"Is Damian all right?" Naomi asked, kneeling by the side of the chair.

"Yes." He turned his head toward her.

"And Valerie?"

"Damian has her," he said, his voice strained, and he sat up again, breathing through clenched teeth like a man in excruciating pain.

The tension coiled in Naomi relaxed.

"What did you do to my arm?" Steve asked, glancing at the oozing wounds.

"I attempted to suck the poison out and used your bottle of Gray Goose to sterilize it the best I could."

His gaze dropped to the tourniquet. "I think you may have saved my life," he said and looked at her. "Ted wasn't so lucky." He grimaced and closed his eyes. "I wasn't... prepared for an attack."

Steve was intentionally blocking my ability to read his mind and see what really happened. I sensed something deeper had occurred, and my gaze dropped to the wounds. He hadn't healed himself. "Why didn't you fix that?" I asked, pointing, and he opened his eyes, meeting my gaze.

"Because when I healed Valerie, my powers transferred to her."

Motion in the room stopped. Even Grace quieted, and everyone stared at Steve.

Shock skittered through my blood, creating an uncomfortable warmth that painted every cell in my body in a suffocating squeeze. "What?"

"I figured it would be easier transporting a healthy woman and not someone still listed in serious condition," he said, meeting my gaze. "So, I was a little preoccupied with the results of doing that when they struck." His eyes dropped to the floor and Jennifer kissed his cheek. "I didn't know if I was going to make it back," he whispered and glanced at her.

"She stole your powers?"

He shook his head. "No, it was more like what happened between Eric and me. Completely unintentional and a hell of a surprise."

"Like when I healed you in Georgia?" Jennifer asked.

"Exactly, except she passed out," Steve said and reached his good hand to the makeshift tourniquet, unhooking the belt. He winced and continued, "At least I'm a black belt. Even with their strength, it gave me enough of an advantage to defend myself. I thought for sure I was dead when that shit bit me."

It took Naomi a good five minutes of sucking, spitting, and sterilizing before she stopped. I met his gaze.

"How did you get away?" I asked. My brain stalled at the fact Steve wasn't supercharged anymore. He had been that way since my father died thirteen years ago and I wondered how he would do being normal.

"Ted," he said. "That bastard drained him while I was trying to figure out how the hell to get Valerie out of his reach before I died from the virus burning in my arm. If Damian hadn't shown up when he did, that thing would have done the same to me. Valerie never woke to witness the attack. She was still unconscious when Damian took Ted's car keys and phone and scooped her up. The last thing I saw before I opened my eyes here were giant talons holding her body as he jumped from the window."

Naomi's eyes glazed with tears and the sudden swell of sorrow in her heart blanketed me. I stepped to her and wrapped her in a warm hug. She allowed it and I ran my hand over the back of her head, whispering "shh" in her ear as she openly cried. Grace joined her, pulling my attention to the infant in Raven's arms.

Naomi pulled away from me, wiping her face. She reached for Grace and Raven gave the baby to her mother. The child snuggled under Naomi's chin, her cries turning to soft whimpers that seemed to soothe her mother's sorrow. Naomi glanced at me and planted a kiss on the back of Grace's head.

"Your friend is going to freak out when she wakes up," I said, and Naomi cracked a smile.

"Valerie doesn't freak out."

Chapter 12

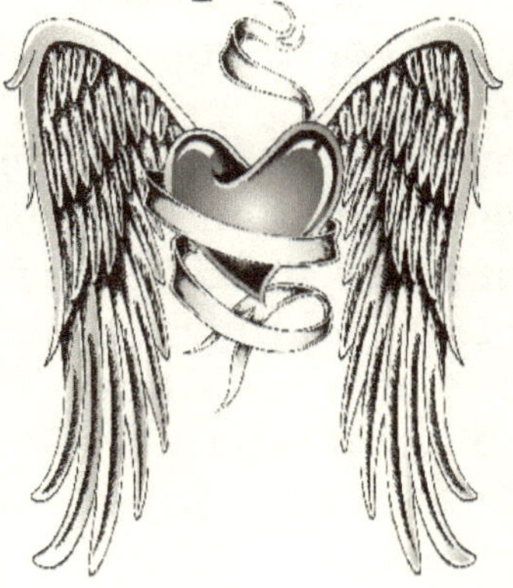

THE MORE I THOUGHT about Naomi's comment, the more intrigued I was to meet this girl.

I collected the guns and set them on the coffee table along with the arsenal of platinum bullets and then grabbed a few beers, handing one to Tom and Steve while Jennifer patched his arm up. He had paled a little after the tourniquet was removed and the blood flow returned to his arm, but he hadn't dropped into a screaming ball on the floor like some of Damian's vampire memories suggested.

Naomi had indeed saved his life and relief loosened the fearful grip on my heart. I'm not sure I could deal with losing Steve on the heels of losing both my father in angel form and Sandy. I said a silent prayer of thanks and traded a glance with Tom, sending a nod in his direction. The tension in his face loosened at my silent acknowledgement of Steve's condition.

Someone upstairs was looking after us tonight.

I picked up the gun, making sure the safety was on before focusing on the back door. The front had the deadbolt on it, and while I knew someone with a vampire's strength could break through it or choose to crash through the windows just as easily, I figured they would come from the direction closest to their victims.

My phone buzzed, and I glanced at the latest requests coming through on Facebook. The number of women in the area sending friend requests was unsettling, and I turned my ringer off. There was no one I wanted to talk to right now. The people I held close were all present in this room and the only other person I might be inclined to talk to knew our home phone number.

Instead of letting my mind drift in that direction, I kept watch out the window and started shuffling through Damian's memories to understand just who Valerie was. Memories tagged with her name came forth in a wave, fronted with Damian's last memory of her as they wheeled her away. Her bloody and pale form sent chills through me, and I was amazed she'd pulled through that ordeal.

Damian knew her from birth until her near death. Only five years had separated them and those were the years he spent in Colorado with Naomi, hiding from the devil. Inspecting the memories, I got a flavor for the girl and only glimpses of the young woman since their return. She was brash and bold and fearless, but even with all she'd been presented with in her life, I was sure the realization of Steve's abilities would throw her for a loop.

I wondered if she got the download of his life as well. I glanced at Steve as he nursed a tall glass of scotch. His hands held a slight tremble and my closer than normal inspection of him pulled his attention away from the television. His eyebrows creased and frustration etched into the new creases in his face. I also noted the appearance of gray at his temples. I guess not having that magic healing mojo really opened the door for aging.

"What?" he asked.

"Did you get the memory transfer as well?" I asked, knowing that was a normal side effect of the power transfers.

He nodded and glanced back at the television, still blocking me.

Before I could press him for details, the wail of a baby set the girls in motion. Before they got to Michael, both Gabriel and Grace had started crying, too. I glanced at the clock, calculating the time since they were last fed. They were going at a clip of two hours between meals. That had to be brutal on Naomi. This time, she chose bottled formula instead of breastfeeding and whether I wanted to admit it; I had a moment of letdown. Tom's face gave away his disappointment as well, and we traded a smirk that Raven didn't catch. If she had, it would have earned him a punch in the arm.

Once the babies were cared for, the cuddle fest started in earnest. I ended up with Gabriel in my arms. He cooed and squeaked and for a few glorious moments I forgot danger lurked. I had never been swayed one way or another as far as children go, but after playing with Gabriel and having him settle into my arms, trusting me enough to fall asleep, my mind was made up. I wanted a child someday, even with the distinct possibility that my child could outshine my unique gift set.

I relinquished a sleeping Gabriel to Jennifer and the three women tucked the children into their car seats, lining them up in full view on the floor in front of the television.

"We'll have to get them cribs," I said as Naomi settled onto the couch across from me.

"Damian already ordered them for the house."
She glanced at the clock on the wall.

I followed her gaze and calculated the timing.
Depending on how fast he was driving and if he
didn't get pulled over for speeding, he should be
home any time now.

"Why hasn't he called?" Worry laced her words.

"He's probably driving like a bat out of hell and
doesn't want to risk their lives by trying to dial
Ted's antiquated flip phone," Steve answered.

Naomi pressed her lips together and nodded.
The mention of Ted's name caused another flare of
pain in her.

"Tell us a little about Valerie," I asked, purposely
trying to keep her mind occupied with something
other than death.

Lights crossed the room, and she popped out of
her seat, running to the window and peering out.
The tickle of a mind scan made me smile, and I
clamped down on my thoughts.

"It's Damian," I said and stood, crossing to the
door and opening it for him, careful not to break
the semi-circle of salt that outlined the entry.

Damian shut the car off and stepped out,
meeting my gaze before walking to the passenger
door. It opened and the sensation of a chill caressed
my skin. I scanned the yard to make sure he was
alone and saw nothing that would explain the
shiver that gripped me. Damian stood with Valerie
in his arms. The thin hospital gown billowed
around her, and each pass of wind brought another
chill, and I realized I was feeling the wind as it blew
against her skin.

Her gaze locked on mine and stayed locked, even
when they crossed the threshold, and I closed the
door. The minute her feet hit the ground, Naomi
was hugging her. Valerie blinked and pushed her

away, staring at Naomi's flat stomach. A whirlwind of thoughts danced in her mind and her eyes saddened.

"She had the babies," Damian said from behind her, and her stunning eyes went wide.

It took me a moment to place where I saw eyes like that and when the answer came, my jaw popped open. Her eyes were the same calico storm as my mother's and Eric's eyes.

"Who's Eric?" Her gaze jumping to me instead of what Damian said and then she shook her head, clearing the diversion, trying to catch up with everything she'd missed.

I didn't bother to answer. Her mind was hitting mach ten, snapping through some of Steve's memories that had been transmitted along with his power. She stared at me, coming up with the answer on her own. The depth of sadness in her eyes shot straight to my heart, like she knew what those memories did to me inside.

Valerie refocused on Naomi's flat stomach, still coming to terms with the progression of memories accosting her. "How long was I out?" she finally asked.

"Not as long as you're thinking," Damian said, and his gaze flicked to mine. A shadow of irritation passed over his features, but nothing broadcast with it. I supposed he wanted to ease her into the different layers of her powers, and I backed off.

"Turning tiger accelerated their growth," Naomi said. "You want to see them?"

The woman blinked. "How long was I out?" she repeated, meeting Naomi's stare. Her scientific mind wasn't able to grasp the tiger angle.

Naomi looked over her head at Damian, trying to calculate the passage of time in her own mind.

Before she could speak the number, Valerie's eyes widened.

"Two weeks? Are you telling me you went from being a little over four weeks pregnant to delivery in two weeks?"

"It was ten days from when the demon attacked you."

She looked at me like I could shed light on the anomaly. I just shrugged, keeping her gaze. A strange sensation crawled under my skin, making my entire form tingle. This was one of Michael's descendants, just like Naomi. A moment of awe encompassed me.

Her confusion seemed to disappear as we stared at each other, and then she blinked and looked away, breaking the overwhelming spell she had over me. She turned and the back of the hospital gown gave me a view of her ass that made me grin.

Damian stepped in front of my view and glared in my direction. This time his glare came with a thought. *"Don't even think about it."*

"Maybe you should get some clothes for Valerie before we parade her into the family room with the rest of the people," Damian said to Naomi.

The blush in Valerie's cheeks heightened, and she reached in back of her, gathering the sides of the hospital gown together, making the gap disappear. When she met my gaze, I couldn't help the grin that stayed plastered on my lips. I looked at the ground and then stepped away, heading into the family room while Naomi retrieved some more appropriate clothing.

When she stepped into the room dressed in jeans and a t-shirt Naomi gave her, and her gaze locked with mine, all thought ceased. She was more stunning than Naomi, and I actually forgot to breathe. The feeling passed as soon as her eyes dropped to the three car seats lining the floor, and Tom nudged me.

I turned my attention to him, and his eyebrow rose in that silent challenge. I rolled my eyes at him, and he covered a smirk with his hand. Sometimes just a look was enough for my brother and me to communicate.

"Did Damian tell you what happened at the hospital?" Steve asked, as Valerie made a beeline to the babies.

She slowed and stopped, the smile on her face fading before she turned toward Steve. "My uncle died?" The question in her voice was enough of an answer, and Steve nodded. Tears filled her pretty eyes, and she turned towards Damian. "Why didn't you tell me?"

"I was concentrating on getting us here as fast as I could," he said.

Her hands shot to her hips and the frown that formed on her lips made me want to cover them with mine. I shoved my hands in my pockets and dropped my gaze to the ground, wondering what the hell was wrong with me.

"Look..." he started.

"Don't give me that shit, Damian. You know I can handle it; you just didn't want to deal with it yourself."

The challenge in her voice drew my gaze back to her, and I focused, reaching into her mind and drawing out some memories she had associated with Damian. I had all of his, along with the overwhelming guilt he felt for ruining her life. Her gaze shifted to me for a moment and then returned to Damian's.

"Why do you constantly feel the need to protect me?" Everyone fell silent. The aggravation projecting from her made everyone shift in their seats.

"Because it's my job," he said. "It has been since you were born."

"Why? Because Michael is my blood?"

"No, because you're *my* blood," he said, staring her down like an overprotective big brother. "And because there's no one else to do it now."

I huffed, breaking the tension and pulling all eyes to me. "She's perfectly capable of protecting herself. Or hadn't you noticed?" I said, but the look in her eyes, and the knowledge that swarmed her brain, made her wobble.

Damian stared at her, blinking like he didn't understand she had all of Steve's gifts. He wasn't there when Steve healed her, and he looked at me. His mouth popped into a little 'o', too preoccupied with this new information to notice Valerie's sway, or the fact her eyes just rolled back in her head.

I was faster than Damian. I caught her as she fell. The moment my skin came in contact with her, it was like being stuck in a wind vortex. Her eyes locked on mine and memories merged. Our powers combined, splitting into destructive and redemptive halves of a coin. I gasped as the darker force melded with my cells, increasing the power within me a thousandfold. The air around her sparkled as the healing forces settled into her and the calico patterns in her eyes swirled.

"Michael's dead?" she asked me, her voice soft and subtle, like a gentle caress.

For the first time in my life, I understood what drove my father to do anything for my mother. I understood the overwhelming connection between my parents. I always thought Sandy was the one, but I was dead wrong.

The woman staring at me with the stormy eyes was my soul mate.

"Yes," I said, and the wind silenced. "So is Lucifer."

She pulled out of my arms and climbed to her feet, sending a glare in Damian's direction. "You could have given me a heads up."

"I figured you'd find out soon enough..." he trailed off. "But if you got his memories like I did, you should have already known," he finished; the unsure crevice between his eyes announced his confusion.

"You should have told me." She gawked at him. "Besides, I didn't just get his memories. I got everyone he's downloaded as well, so how the hell would I know what happened, with the sheer volume of shit in my head?"

She had a point. Steve had my parent's memories, Eric's memories and an assortment of others from his FBI days, and now with twenty-five hundred years of Damian's memories on top of that, there was no rhyme or reason to the flood in his memory banks. It was enough to make you think you were schizophrenic. Now she had mine on top of that, just like I had all the above and hers. I couldn't help the chuckle and she turned that fierce glare in my direction.

"If you look closely enough, you'd know that Damian stole a little piece of my talents," I said. "He can hear your thoughts just as easily as I can."

"Then why can't I hear either of you?"

"I'm a master at blocking people from getting in my head," I grinned, and her eyes narrowed. Her 'fuck you' resounded in my head, although she kept it from escaping her mouth.

Damian smirked. "I figured it out from the memories," he said.

Steve cleared his throat, calling our attention back to him. "CJ, Valerie can have your room tonight. You'll stay down here on the couch."

I know he was just trying to diffuse the budding argument, but the blank stares he received from everyone just left him the focal point of our attention. It was only a little after nine and the real entertainment had just begun.

"I imagine everyone's tired. It's been a hell of a day and I need to get some rest."

Damian's stare dropped to his arm. "You didn't heal that bite yourself like I assumed, did you?"

"No. I didn't," Steve said, and a shadow drew across Damian's face, his eyes jumping to Steve's, looking for signs of the disease overtaking him. "Your wife sucked the poison out and saved my life."

"I figured it was worth a try," Naomi said. "And it worked."

Damian opened his mouth and closed it, his eyebrows arching. He apparently never thought to do something like that. Of course, he was usually the one administering the bite, so it wouldn't dawn on him to suck the poison out, not when his goal was to drain his victims dry.

"I'm going to bed," Steve mumbled and headed upstairs.

Damian's gaze followed Steve, and then he glanced at Jennifer. "Keep an eye on him tonight," he said.

"I thought…"

"He probably is, but just in case, keep an eye on him. If he spikes a fever or starts hallucinating, come get me."

"Actually, come get me," Valerie interrupted. "I'm the one in med school."

Jennifer looked between the two of them and nodded, taking her leave as well.

Instead of dwelling on the situation, Valerie refocused on the babies, crouching down and running the tips of her fingers over each little face, mesmerized by their perfection.

"Naomi, your children are beautiful," she said, looking over her shoulder.

"Thank you," she said and promptly yawned. "I think we'll take them upstairs and try to get some sleep before they wake up again," she said, and Damian hesitated, leveling a glare in my direction.

"I'm not a child, Damian," Valerie said.

"I know you're not, but I don't trust him." He pointed at me.

Valerie rolled her eyes, which only endeared me to her more. "Go help your wife with your children," she ordered, pointing toward the stairs.

He only hesitated a moment and then he grabbed the last two car seats, following Naomi upstairs, leaving the four of us alone in the family room. I waited for a minute and then turned to Valerie.

"Hi, I'm CJ," I said, putting my hand out and going through the formalities that Damian forgot.

"I know," she said, but took my hand anyway. "Do you mind if I call you Chris? I like that better than your nickname."

Her grip was firm and warm and sure, and even though Sandy was the only one to ever call me by my real name, I smiled and nodded in response. "This is my brother Tom, and his wife Raven," I waved to the two of them on the couch and Valerie exchanged handshakes and salutations before taking a seat in the chair that Steve vacated. She quietly studied her hands.

"I'm sorry for your loss," Raven said, her Irish lilt presenting itself.

Valerie tried to smile, but a tear belied the attempt, sliding down her cheek and making me want to hold her and wipe the sorrow out of her eyes.

Raven moved first, taking Valerie's hands, her eyes sincere and warm, welcoming Valerie to the family without words. I knew Valerie was close with Naomi, but I had a feeling Raven would be her ultimate confidant. Raven had a way of keeping secrets, even from Steve and me, and I think it had to do with some of her weird wiccan hexes, either that or Tom taught her the basics of blocking thought, which probably made more sense, but I was never sure.

As far as a sister-in-law goes, she was pretty cool, and she made Tom happy, so I dealt with the natural separation that had occurred between Tom and me as he relied on her more and more. Valerie seemed to take to her as well and ended up in her arms, while Tom and I sat by like awkward onlookers.

When her tears dried, she pulled away and wiped her face. "I'm sorry."

"Don't be," I said, thinking about how badly I'd handled my most recent loss. A brief bout of tears was as graceful as it gets compared to my complete meltdown. She met my gaze and offered a half-hearted smile.

"Did you want me to show you where you're sleeping?" I asked.

"In a little while. I'm not tired right now," she said.

"Tom and I are heading up, and I'll leave you some pajamas and a change of clothes for the morning," Raven said. "Maybe we can go shopping tomorrow to get you whatever you need."

"Thank you," Valerie said, and we watched them head upstairs. She turned to me. "You wouldn't have a laptop, would you?"

"Yes." I said and left her alone in the family room while I ran up to my room. While I was up there, I grabbed a sheet, blanket and pillow for the couch and brought that downstairs along with my laptop, piling the bedding on the loveseat before handing her the laptop.

"Mind if I turn on the television?"

"Go ahead. I need to see just how far behind I've gotten with all this." She waved at her side and propped open the laptop.

I studied her profile with the remote in my hand, forgetting about the television and she sighed, sliding her gaze to me. Her fingers paused over the keyboard. Her exasperation with my acute observation of her made me smile.

"I'm sorry." I turned the television on, feeling her eyes still on me.

"How much of my life did you see?" she asked, pulling my attention back to hers.

"All of it. The same as you saw of mine."

She nodded and refocused on the computer. Her forehead creased in concentration, ignoring me as she tabbed through the assignment list. Finally, she snapped the laptop closed and handed it to me.

"Making up two weeks of classes and labs is going to kill me," she muttered and ran her hands through her hair. "Never mind internship hours." Her arms crossed and her frown deepened. "I hate demons," she added, turning her glare in my direction. "They always seem to fuck up my life just when I think I have my shit together."

I laughed and put the remote on the table. Instead of agreeing with her, I stood, crossing to the sliders, staring out at the cold evening. The demons I had encountered were more interested in seduction than destruction. But maybe that was by design. I wasn't cut from an angelic bloodline like she was. However, Lucifer wanted me just as much as he coveted the offspring of angels. My smile faded as shadows stretched under the moonlight. I took a couple of steps away from the door and closed my eyes, building a barrier around the house like I had once done around our car when I was four. Any beast that tried to reach the house would fry like a bug in a bug zapper.

I thought the scale would be a problem, but with the darkness fully charged inside me, it was much easier than protecting the car had been. I knew it would stop a human. I just hoped like hell it would stop whatever monsters Lucifer commanded.

Valerie stepped next to me, staring out at the moon playing on the water. "It's beautiful here," she said.

"It's home."

Her silence pulled me out of the trance I'd put myself in, and I glanced at her.

"You look like Damian."

"You look like Naomi," I countered.

"She's blood, so it makes sense, but you and Damian aren't related, so it's a little weird. Of course, your hair isn't nearly as dark, but your eyes are the same striking blue."

"Striking?"

She smiled, and I felt a need stir inside me and it had nothing to do with my heart, or soul, for that matter.

"You really let a demon tie you up?" Dimples appeared in her cheeks and mine bloomed with heat.

I shifted, focusing back on the darkness beyond the glass, suddenly uncomfortable and unable to look at her. I swore my face must be the shade of a bright red kickball. "I wasn't exactly myself," I said without looking at her.

She chuckled.

The kind of chuckle that was meant as a turn on and I slid my gaze to her. "You like your men tied up?" I raised an eyebrow. It was her turn to blush, and she grinned, shrugging and looking back outside. Before I could explore more of this conversation, she paled and took a step back, dragging me with her.

There must have been a dozen pale creatures slinking across the backyard. I gave her hand that gripped my upper arm a gentle pat and she turned her frightened gaze to me.

"They won't get through." My voice held confidence, but deep inside, I was trembling just as much as she was. Damian, Steve, and I had wiped out more than this at the cove, but that was three of us and, of course, Paradise Cove probably had a lot to do with it.

We both focused on the approaching horde and, without thinking, I slung my arm around Valerie's shoulder and pulled her close. It was time to concentrate on the deadly quality of the wall I put up. I wasn't sure of how much sizzle to put into it.

"I want to see them burn," Valerie said, answering my silent contemplation, and a chill ran up my spine.

She had every right to hate these creatures as much as demons, and I concentrated, glaring at the approaching danger. Saliva ran from their lips and their teeth gleamed in the moonlight. My heart pounded in my chest, sending throbbing vibrations through my skin. The harder my heart beat, the hungrier the approaching vampires looked.

"Just a few more feet," I muttered, focusing on the entire perimeter of the house because I wasn't as much of an idiot as they thought. This wasn't the only line of assault. Still, when they advanced, I took a cautious step backward, pulling Valerie with me. The power inside me grew and I couldn't tell whether it was the adrenaline or the power raking across my skin like a hundred finely manicured nails. The sensation grew, moving from the land of pleasure into the world of discomfort, and I gritted my teeth.

"Come on, you motherfuckers," I growled, loud enough for their acute hearing to pick up. I moved Valerie behind me and positioned myself in a fighting stance, waving them in with my leading hand. The results were memorable.

They all launched towards the glass slider and the moment they hit my invisible barrier, each vampire burst into a ball of flame. The roar of fire drowned out their screams, but I heard them, and the dark part of my soul reveled in it.

Valerie let out a high-pitched laugh, and I glanced back at her, smiling.

She met my gaze with a measure of awe. "The only one I ever saw do something that impressive was Michael."

Being compared to an archangel was humbling, and I glanced outside at the black dust that spun on the wind. "I'm not an angel."

"Oh, I gathered that." She stepped away.

I turned towards her. "What do you mean by that?"

"You're more recent activities?"

I shoved my hands into my pockets and stared at the floor, shamed by the fact she was privy to my more decadent actions. Instead of apologizing, I lifted my gaze to hers, studying her memories of past events, especially the times after the more traumatic events. Naomi was right about one thing. The girl never freaked out. Ever.

And therein lay the challenge.

I let a grin slowly surface and narrowed my eyes, stepping closer. "So, you want to try out some of those 'activities' with me?"

She laughed. The kind of laugh that bruised a man's ego and when she went into the gale realm, I crossed my arms, my good humor turning sourer by the second. I didn't have anywhere to storm off to. I was tempted to tell her she could sleep on the couch, but I knew Steve would be pissed.

"You know I'm rich, right?" I said, feeling more than just a bruised ego now. Most girls threw themselves at me, but this one was aloof in a way that pissed me off.

Somehow, my comment made her laugh even harder. "I couldn't give a rat's ass how much money you have," she sputtered through the laughter and settled into the couch, holding her stomach as her laughter wound down.

I didn't know what to do. Being rejected had been a truly foreign concept until Sandy cut me loose and it just didn't seem natural.

"I'm sorry if I hurt your ego," she said with the light of humor still dancing in her eyes.

"Right," I said, delivering the sarcasm I was famous for before stalking to the refrigerator to grab a beer. "You want one?" I asked.

"Sure," she said.

I wasn't sure why I still wanted to be in her presence, especially after that harsh shoot down, but I did, just like a pathetic puppy following its master around, hoping for a treat. I grabbed a beer for her and returned to the couch. After I switched the television on and opened the beers, I handed her both the beer and the remote, settling into the far side of the couch.

"You don't have to stay," she said, and I raised my eyebrows, waving at the linens on the other couch. She was the one encroaching on my temporary bedroom.

"Oh, sorry." She took a sip of beer and the mad shuffle through the channels began and I glanced at her after two rounds of channel changing.

"Make up your mind."

The glare she shot me made me raise my hands in surrender. She finally snapped the box off and tossed the remote on the table. When she brought her beer to her lips, her hand was shaking. She noticed too and put the beer on the table.

"Are you okay?"

She just stared at her hands in her lap, her hair obscuring my view of her face. I reached out and pushed her hair back.

"Oh, babe," I whispered at the sight of her tear-stained cheeks. When her gaze met mine, I felt her world crumbling around her and moved closer, pulling her to my chest. She covered her face and leaned into me, silently crying. Losing her uncle hit harder than she expected.

When her shaking stopped, I threaded my fingers through her hair with my palms gently pressed to each cheekbone and pulled her away from my chest. Her misty eyes met mine and I couldn't help it. I leaned in for a kiss. Instead of her lips, like I intended, her fingers pressed against my lips, and she moved out of my grip.

"No."

Such a simple word, but devastating in its own right.

"Why not?"

"Because everyone I come to care about dies."

Stunned to the point of silence, I just stared at her. I knew the feeling, but I'd rebelled against it for so long that I just couldn't accept the reason. Hell, I felt the attraction, her attraction, not just mine, and I leaned back. The fact that she was scared didn't negate the sting.

"And if I promised I wouldn't die?"

"Michael, the archangel, died. What hope do you have if he can be destroyed?"

"Michael's not dead, he's just locked in heaven. Just like Lucifer is locked in hell," I said. "Damian saw to that, and Lucifer was *possibly* the only force on this planet that could have destroyed me, and I'm not a hundred percent sure even he could have." I knew it sounded cocky as hell, but it was the truth.

"You're not a god."

"No shit. I bleed when I'm cut and break when I'm punched. I'm flesh and blood, just like you."

"I can't take the chance," she whispered, piling onto my frustration.

"I know damned well you feel the current between us just as acutely as I do," I said, and the sincerity in her eyes morphed to anger.

"It doesn't matter."

"What? Are you going to insulate yourself from all human emotions? Just wall it up and become a walking zombie?"

"Fuck you! You know nothing about me," she spit out, leaning towards me in her anger.

I laughed and tapped my temple. "Oh, yes, I do." I mentally yanked her toward me. Unfortunately, I yanked a little too hard and our foreheads met, dazing both of us.

"Ouch." She held her forehead.

I covered the sting of mine as well and met her gaze.

"Smooth, CJ," she said and broke into a genuine smile.

I started laughing, and she followed. As they say, the third time is the charm, and this time I didn't mentally or physically man-handle her. I just leaned in and kissed her cheek, tasting the dried-up tears on her skin.

"Thank you," I whispered on her skin.

She turned her lips into mine and the first genuine attempt was sweet and awkward and nothing like I imagined. I pulled back, meeting her gaze and the second time we closed the distance, not just with our mouths, but our bodies, like molded magnets, came together with all the pent-up electricity sparking between us. She felt damned good in my arms, and I lost track of time, of where we were and of everything else that happened in the last few days. I fell into blissful nothingness where only her tongue reigned.

She broke the kiss first, and I pulled away, settling onto the couch, forcing my breathing back to normal. Kissing Sandy didn't consume me the way that kiss did, and I stared at the dark television, wrestling with the urge to tear every stitch of clothing off her.

"Maybe that's what I need," she said, and my head snapped in her direction.

"I'm a guy, don't tempt me," I said, running my hand through my hair, unsure if she was serious or not. I also knew Steve was no longer privy to what was in my head, and she was supposed to be sleeping in my bed, anyway.

"What if I said I really wanted to tie you up?" she grinned, her eyes sparkling with the type of mischief I knew would land me in a world of trouble.

I crawled the few feet toward her, pushing her down on the couch under me. "What if I wanted to tie *you* up?" I said and didn't wait for an answer. I settled on top of her and licked her sweet lips again. They parted, and I dropped into heaven.

Before I knew it, both our shirts were balled up on the floor and I was exploring the bounty of her chest with my mouth. God, she was delicious, and I moved my way back up her neck to her lips. This kiss was slow and seductive and playful and damned if I wasn't harder than an oak tree.

I wanted it all, every inch of her soft skin. I wanted to drink her like wine, and I wanted her delectable mouth to swallow every inch of me. When the kiss broke, I stared into her stormy calico eyes and pulled away.

With the want still pounding through my veins, I said. "You need to go to bed."

"What?" she asked.

Her voice carried the husky rasp of lust, and I almost gave in, ripping the rest of her clothes off and just taking her here. But this was not a rush fuck.

Valerie deserved better than that. Besides, if I screwed her here on the couch, letting the frantic need in both of us loose, it would be the end of whatever started here tonight.

"You need to go upstairs before we do something you'll regret in the morning." I couldn't believe I was being the voice of reason, and she certainly didn't take too kindly to it. She huffed and put her shirt on, except it wasn't her shirt, it was mine, but I don't think she figured it out until she was upstairs and by then, I was sure she was too mad to come back down.

I folded her shirt neatly on the table along with my jeans before tucking the sheet around the couch cushions. I crossed to the downstairs bathroom and splashed cold water on my face to tame the hunger still present. The hunger that almost made me march upstairs, consequences be damned, but the chill of the icy splash tempered it. The fact I didn't act on my impulses tonight gave me hope I wasn't a total jackass.

I stretched out on the couch, concentrating on the barrier around the house, willing it to remain until the sunlight broke the horizon.

Chapter 13

THE SCRUNCHING OF BAGS pulled me out of sleep and I wiped the drool off my chin and turned onto my back, covering my eyes with my forearm. "What time is it?"

"It's a little after three," Steve's voice announced from nearby.

"In the afternoon?" I tilted my head back, peering under my arm. Steve was seated in his recliner with the newspaper in his hands. He glanced in my direction and nodded. I sat up and rubbed my face. "Why didn't someone wake me?"

"Valerie said you held a force field around the house until dawn. I figured you needed the sleep." He folded the paper.

I scanned the kitchen for the noises that woke me and found it empty. I swung my legs over the side of the couch. "Where is everyone?"

"The girls just came back from shopping. Tom's working out, and I have no idea where Damian went." He stared at me. "Interesting combination there." He pointed his chin toward the folded clothing and tossed the paper onto the side table.

I said nothing. Instead, I reached for the jeans and slipped them on before I got out from under the covers. "Do we know how long we'll have house guests?" I asked, folding the blankets neatly. The answer would drive whether I stowed these in the washing machine or on the ottoman in the corner of the room for tonight.

"I don't know, but Jen extended the invitation for them to stay until they close on their house. She seems to enjoy helping with the babies."

"Raven likes helping, too," I said, and then headed to my room to get a clean pair of clothing. Without thinking, I opened my door and got an eyeful of satin and lace.

"Get out!" Raven snapped, but it wasn't her I was staring at.

Valerie turned towards me in only a bra and panties. I wasn't sure if the dress she held was going on or coming off, but I didn't care. The view was outstanding.

"Christopher James," Raven said again, calling my attention away from Valerie.

I blinked and stepped into the room. "I need a change of clothes. Besides, she's got more coverage than some of the chicks we see on the beach." I didn't wait for the okay. Instead, I crossed to my dresser, pulling out a pair of jeans and clean underwear before walking out. It took everything I had not to try for another quick glance before the door closed behind me.

I dialed the shower into the warm zone and stripped, stepping in after brushing my teeth and using the toilet. The soap smelled fresher this morning than I remembered, and I wondered if it was just the fact I had a good night's sleep or if it was something else heightening my senses. I mused over that while I did my hair and then I just stood under the spray with my palms on the cool tile, letting the water cascade down my back. The sensation was hypnotizing.

The curtain rattled and my eyes snapped open. I stood, getting a face full of water, and coughed out the spray that had gone into my mouth. Valerie tilted her head at me.

"Since you decided walking in on me was okay, I thought I'd take my turn at getting an eyeful."

She went to close the curtain, and I grabbed her wrist, pulling her under the spray with me before she could escape. The jeans and t-shirt she'd donned soaked through in seconds and I raised an eyebrow.

"Chris!" she shrieked and tried to break my grip.

"You made the questionable decision to come into the bathroom. You're fair game now." I pushed her into the corner and blocked her escape from the warm water by planting my arms on either side of her. "Want to play doctor?" I said and grinned.

She smacked my chest, and the corners of her lips twitched into an unwanted smile. "Don't be an ass. Just let me out of here."

I glanced at her wet attire. "I think you'll have to take that off in here. No sense in dripping all across the house." I was enjoying this game.

She reached for the controls, and I gasped when the water turned frigid, jumping away from her and out of the spray.

"That was mean," I said, and she flashed a wicked grin at me and slid out of the shower, leaving me to dance around the cold spray in order to turn off the water. When I pushed the curtain aside, I fully expected an empty bathroom. Instead, Valerie was peeling her jeans off.

She turned and threw the wet denim at me.

"You mind hanging those from the shower rod for me?" The grin that danced on her lips was enough to spark an interest, and it didn't go unnoticed. I dropped the jeans on the floor and reached for the towel, but she snatched it off the rack first.

"Uh-uh. 'Mr. I'm too sexy for my shirt'. Hang the pants first, then maybe I'll give you the towel."

Damn it all to hell. Now I was self-conscious and aware I was naked and responding to being near her. My lack of control was embarrassing, and she was enjoying toying with me the way I had toyed with her in the shower.

I scooped up the wet fabric and wrung it out over the shower drain and neatly hung it from the curtain bar before turning back to her.

"You have an exceptionally nice ass," she grinned and handed me the towel.

I chuckled and rolled my eyes, even though her brazenness caught me off guard and my face flushed with heat. "So do you," I said, and wrapped the towel around my waist.

She peeled off her shirt and tossed it to me. "Can you hang that as well?"

I wrung the shirt out and repeated hanging it neatly over the bar. When I turned back, she had a towel wrapped around her and two more wet garments that she deposited in my hand before leaving me with her soaking underwear. I slung them over the rod and shut the bathroom door.

This time I locked it.

Chapter 14

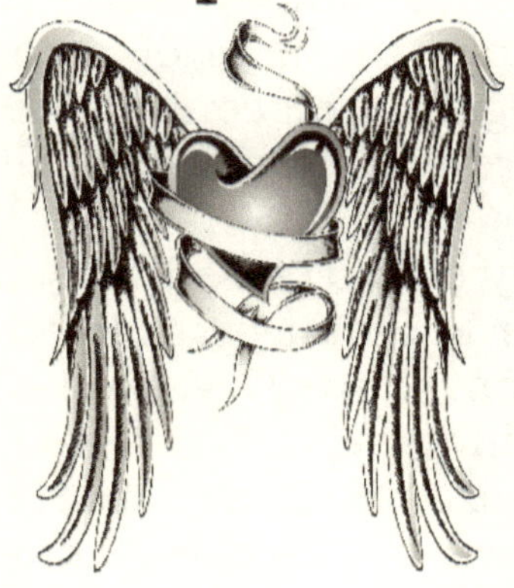

I DIDN'T REALIZE I could strut, but that's exactly what I did. I fucking strutted with my shirt hanging open, right up to Valerie and Naomi, standing by the refrigerator. The game was on, and I didn't care who took notice. I reached for the handle, pulling the ice box open and reached for a soda. When I closed the refrigerator, I faced Valerie with a hint of a grin.

I didn't wait for a reaction, instead I ducked back into the family room and switched on the television, propping my feet up on the table. I cracked the can open and the stupid thing sprayed all over me. I couldn't believe it and the incessant laughing behind me told me they saw it too, so I couldn't just brush it off.

Steve snorted laughter, looking at me over his Kindle like I was the world's biggest idiot. I guess my dating practices were rusty, hell; they were non-existent, and this was all trial and error on my part. I had Sandy for fifteen years and never had to try to get a girl before, and now I just looked like a ridiculous peacock ruffling his feathers.

I guess I missed the 'how to be cool' class in high school, and it certainly wasn't on the college curriculum. I took the hem of my shirt and wiped my face, settling into the couch with no intention of calling any more attention to myself than I already had.

I had already embarrassed myself to the point of no return. Their laughter just sealed my fate.

"Oh, come on, Chris?" Valerie said. "Can't you see the humor in this?"

I slid my gaze to Steve, and he was silently laughing so hard his face was red. "Fuck you," I whispered, and he pointed his finger at me, the admonishment for my language lost in his laughter.

"What'd I miss?" Raven asked, stepping into the family room.

"CJ thought he'd be all cool and cocky until he opened his soda and it sprayed all over him," Steve said, his laughter winding down.

Raven smiled, but God bless her, she didn't laugh.

"It's really okay to laugh," I said. "It was funny."

"I won't laugh at your sad attempt to woo the girl," she said, waving toward Valerie and, as only Raven can, she silenced the room for exactly three heartbeats, and then laughter erupted.

As for me, I ducked down farther into the couch, wishing like hell I could disappear. Valerie came into view, and I met her gaze when she squatted in front of me.

"What?"

She smirked and raised an eyebrow. *Do I have to go get some rope?*

The question resounded in my head, and I clamped my lips together against a smirk. *Maybe.* I sent the thought back and received an all-out grin.

"Want to go grab something to eat?" she asked me directly, and my smile faded.

"When Damian gets back, I'd love to go grab some food with you." My gaze flicked to the sliders and back and her smile disappeared.

"We're never going to be safe, are we?" Naomi asked.

I turned and stared at Naomi. "I don't know, but you're a hell of a lot more prepared now than you were before you met us."

"What about me?" Valerie said.

"It's my personal mission in life to make sure you're safe," I said.

"Now *that's* how you woo a girl," Raven said, pointing at me.

I glanced up at her in the darkest way possible, broadcasting just by way of my expression, for her to shut the hell up. She chuckled and disappeared into the workout room to find her husband. My quiet and borderline boring home had now become a mecca of activity and I just wanted the quiet back.

As if reading my mind, the three babies started crying all at once.

"For the love of..." I didn't finish the sentence; instead, I trudged up to my room and closed the door, throwing myself on my neatly made bed.

The creak of the door interrupted my mope, and I turned, staring at the last person I wanted to see. Valerie shut the door and crossed, taking a seat next to me, and I turned my head toward the wall. I didn't want to give her the satisfaction of seeing my full-blown irritation.

"What you said was really sweet."

I grunted my response.

"I'm not very good at this dating thing," she admitted, and I rolled to my side, facing her and propping myself up on my elbow.

"I obviously suck at it," I said.

"Not really. It's quite entertaining." She smiled in that emboldened way that made me want to strip her down again.

"You realize when you smile at me like that, I just want to rip your clothes off."

She shrugged. "You've only known me for less than a day."

"I'm aware of that, but the memory sharing shit makes it seem like I've known you all my life." I reached up and tucked the stray strands of hair behind her ear. "Which is kind of a mind fuck, you know?"

"A big-time mind fuck," she agreed. "Especially since I think love at first sight is a crock of shit."

We stared at each other for a moment, and then her words sank in. "I wasn't a believer either. Sandy and I knew each other since we were born and at first, she annoyed the hell out of me, but then my father died, and she was there and for the first time I saw her as an individual and not as Uncle Danny's annoying kid."

Her brow creased, and I gave her the time to inspect my memories. When she made the correct connections that told her he was only an uncle by name and not relations, her features relaxed.

"I know, weird as hell, but we always called him Uncle Danny. I don't think my mother knew how to explain all the connections she had before my dad."

"She hurt you," Valerie said and threaded her fingers through mine.

"Yes. And I did not handle it well." I sighed. "I'm still not handling things well."

"You're a smart guy. You'll figure it out." She gave me a smirk, and I squeezed her hand.

"You know…"

"I know. You're a genius and you're richer than God and you've got mega-freaky powers that could blow this earth to bits as easily as you dispatched of those vampires. But here's the thing, I really don't care about those things."

I opened my mouth, and she put her finger over my lips, stopping my retort.

"What I do care about is how you treat others. How you conduct yourself in life. Why do you think I went to medical school?"

"To help kids," I said. I didn't need to search her memories for answers. I had already taken a long look while night crawled into dawn.

"So, let me ask you a question. Besides teaching Karate class once a week, what exactly do you want to do with your life?"

I stared at her and shrugged. I had no clue of what I wanted to do. I had a computer science degree and tooled around putting together video games for giggles, but nothing serious and she was right. I had more money than I knew what to do with and Tom and Raven could have moved out a long time ago, but this was home, and the only remaining connection Tom had to our parents.

They had discussed moving into the house on Nubble Road when the current lease ran out, but that wasn't for another four months, and Steve and Jen hadn't broached the subject about moving to either New York or their place in New Hampshire. I think they were waiting until Sandy and I got married.

"I will figure something out." I didn't want to discuss what my future held. I kind of liked doing what I wanted, when I wanted. But I also love teaching the little kids how to defend themselves. "Maybe I'll increase the number of classes I teach," I added.

Her eyes pierced through me and without speaking, she passed judgment on me.

"I told you, I'm not an angel."

"I know, but you could do so much with your gifts," she started, and I shut her down.

"If word ever got out, you think I'd ever be safe? You think governments would allow me to roam free?" I shook my head. "They'd hunt me down hoping to lock me up until I agreed to become their weapon of mass destruction. If you think it's bad running from demons and vampires, try adding the vilest of humans to that list."

Her face paled as the realization came to her. The reality that her power was not for public consumption hit and with it, the hopes of healing the world crashed and burned.

"If you decide to help someone, you can't blatantly do it. Look at Steve's memories, on how he used the healing power. Granted, he wasn't a doctor, but he saved a few people in his stint as an FBI agent."

"But..." she started and closed her mouth. Her mind filtered to a scene from a movie she once watched, where hordes of people bombarded a famed healer. "I'd become a sideshow trick, wouldn't I?"

I nodded, and she hung her head. "I just want to help sick kids."

I hooked my finger under her chin and forced her to look at me. "You still can. You just have to use medicine unless the only way to save them is by using the power."

"Assuming I still have it," she said, and I grinned.

"I think it's probably safe to assume you'll have it for a while." I pushed myself up and pulled her into a gentle kiss. When the kiss broke, the colors in her eyes swirled, slowing and settling as the air cooled between us.

"You really know how to fuck with my mind," she said.

"I love it when you talk dirty," I purred, wrapping my arms around her waist and shifting her onto her back. "Now, I think you may have mentioned... bondage?"

She laughed and wrapped her hands around my wrists and spread her arms wide. I surrendered and let her hold my arms in place. I found the curve of her neck and nibbled. She giggled under me, and I slid my gaze from her throat to her eyes. My playfulness faded, replaced by the certainty that she would be beyond fantastic in bed.

Her cheeks bloomed, and she smiled at me. "I'd be the best you ever had," she said.

I thought about the wild drug induced sex fest of the last few days and raised an eyebrow.

"I'd still be the best," she said, but this time the conviction waned.

"I'm thinking you're full of shit," I said, twisting my arms from her grip and wrapped them around her. "Remember, I have all your memories," I whispered in her ear. "My little virgin girl."

I pulled back and grinned.

Her smile faltered. "You knew?" she asked, and then she rolled her eyes. "Of course you knew."

"Yes. I knew. And I could have been an insensitive bastard last night, too, but I'm not. I was never like Tom, or my father, for that matter." I pecked her lips and propped up on my elbows. "Although I went to Jenna's houses for some action. I just didn't expect the triplets from hell, and I can't lie. The physical side of the equation was out of this world, but it wasn't worth the shitty feeling the next day."

"The walk of shame?"

"Yep. Sucks," I said and slid off her, propping up on my elbow again.

"You don't think I'm a freak for—"

I shook my head before she finished. "You had your reasons, and I respect that."

She stared at me for a while and did a pretty good job at blocking her thoughts.

"I don't understand how she could let you go?"

"Sandy?"

"Yes."

"Well, I think it was a couple of things. Distance being one and her father being the other driver. You see, her father hated my father. I can't really blame him, either. My father was diabolical in his younger years until he kidnapped my mother." I sighed and fell on my back, staring at the ceiling. "My dad did some pretty messed up things, and it poisoned Sandy's father's opinion of me. He tolerated me until he caught us in bed together. Ironically, that was our first time."

She chuckled, scanning over the memory. "You are so lucky he didn't own a gun."

"I know." I couldn't help but smile. Sandy's father had had one major conniption. I propped myself up and stared at Valerie. "Damian has a gun. Should I be worried about him popping a cap in my ass?"

"Are you planning on popping my cherry?" she asked, an impish glint danced in her eyes.

I laughed. "I think that may be a distinct possibility."

"Then I think you'll have to battle Damian for my honor." She batted her eyes at me and grinned like the Cheshire cat just as the door swung open.

"What the hell do you think you're doing?"

"Speak of the devil," I said, and his nostrils flared. Damian had a protective streak a mile wide where Valerie was concerned, and seeing her in a nearly compromising position didn't help my case.

"Get off her," he growled.

"I'm not 'on' her," I countered, and when she went to get up, I pressed my hand to her shoulder, holding her in place. I glanced at her. "Do you want to get up?"

Her eyes darted to Damian, and she shrugged. "It might be best."

I lifted my hand and let her go. As soon as she was out the door, I sat up and leveled a glare at Damian. "I wasn't doing anything with her."

"Damned right," he said.

His macho, high-and-mighty attitude needed to be taken down a few pegs, and I hopped to my feet. "If I was, there isn't a goddamned thing you could do about it."

Damian stepped farther into the room and closed the door behind him before turning towards me. Aggravation tensed the muscles in his jaw and narrowed both his eyes and lips.

"You're crossing a line," he growled, and I grinned.

"And here I thought you'd breathe a sigh of relief, considering your massive insecurities where your wife is concerned." I knew I was poking the bear, but I needed some release for the building anger inside me. And who better to take it out on than someone on an equal plane?

The mental shove came, and I stepped back, catching myself in a ready stance. "You don't really want to wage that kind of war with me." I warned. If I let go on that front, I'm not sure if anyone would be left standing, and Damian reconsidered.

He glanced around the room and then directly at me. "Backyard," he said through clenched teeth.

"After you," I waved at the door.

He hesitated a moment and then turned and I followed. It was going to feel really good pummeling the shit out of him. He sent a glare over his shoulder as he rounded the corner and, with a sweep of his hand, the sliders opened. We passed by the rest of the family, leaving them staring with slack jaws.

I closed the door behind me in the same manner as he opened it. The patio bricks were cold on my bare feet and the air settled a chill over me. Damian slipped off his shoes, tossing them by the lounge chairs, and turned on me.

I shifted to the ready, waving him in like I had the vampires the night before. His face turned red, and he stepped forward, taking on the same form. When his face transformed into a grin, I had a second to wonder if this was a wise decision.

I could almost hear my father saying "Hajime!" and we both stepped into the ring. With my thoughts blocked, I let myself react. Damian threw a punch, and I parried, stepping in and pulling him off balance. He recovered in time to counter my foot sweep and he spun out of my hold. His foot came around and before I could block it, he connected with my abdomen, sucking the air from my lungs and knocking me on my ass.

I scrambled to my feet, forcing my breath in slowly, ignoring the throbbing pain in my diaphragm. He didn't let me catch my breath and launched into his next attack and damned if he wasn't fast. I blocked nearly everything and finally an opportunity presented itself and I hooked his arm, rolling him over my hip and onto his back, and I remembered to let go instead of protecting him like I would have in the dojo. His breath escaped in an 'oaf' as he hit the slate square, his head bouncing on the hard stone before he could stop it.

His daze only lasted a moment, and he sat up, climbing to his feet. He glanced at the sliders, at the audience I knew was there but refused to focus on, and that was a grave mistake. I spun and my foot connected with his chest, knocking him on his back. This time, he didn't get up right away. He blinked and wheezed, staring at the sky before his gaze traveled to me.

"Shit," he coughed and rolled onto his knees, slowly getting to his feet. "That's going to leave a bruise," he said.

"Never. Ever. Take your eyes off your sparring partner." I pointed at him. "First fucking rule, dude. First fucking rule." I gave a quick bow and walked away. I had the benefit of the reflection on the glass, so when he launched his next attack, I got the drop on him, ducking under his kick and sweeping his leg out from under him.

I hopped to my feet and stared down at him with enough distance between us to counter any strike he attempted.

"Are you done yet?" I asked, knowing just how frustrated he was. After all, I was just this twenty-four-year-old kid, and he was closer to three thousand years old.

"You need to stay away from Valerie," he said from his position on the ground.

I laughed and the door behind me opened.

"Are you two done with your testosterone contest?"

I didn't turn towards Valerie, not with Damian still in fight mode. When her hand landed on my arm, I met her gaze.

"Enough," she said, and I relaxed, dropping my hands to my sides.

Damian got to his feet, and I bowed out, turning and heading back inside, leaving her to deal with him. As I passed Steve, I got a nod of approval, which meant I did well on my forms. It meant a lot coming from him, since he picked up teaching Tom and me when my father died.

I knew Damian had studied several arts under some of the most talented masters over the millenniums, but he'd never studied under *my* mentors.

Chapter 15

I LEANED AGAINST THE wall with the silent square in my hand, waiting for it to light up and vibrate, announcing a table was available. I glanced at the gorgeous brunette sitting on the bench, her calico eyes scanning the crowd like she expected an assassin to jump out. I leaned close to her ear.

"I promise, you're safe tonight."

Valerie met my gaze and offered a tight smile.

"I promise."

The second time seemed to ease her mind a little and the stress in her shoulders relaxed.

"How'd you convince him to let us go out alone?"

Her lips stretched into a smile. "I told him it was his turn to man up. You stood watch last night and deserved some down time. When he argued about you having enough downtime, I said I wanted dinner and you had offered."

"So, you basically told him he had no choice."

"That sounds about right."

"I'm sure he wasn't happy." I focused on the crowd again. The unit in my hand buzzed, and I showed her. "Our table." I waited for her to stand

and gather her coat and purse before approaching the hostess.

When we were seated, Valerie sighed. "I don't want to be your rebound."

The softness in her voice tore at my chest. I damned well didn't want that and instead of agreeing; I focused on the wood grains in the table, questioning my intentions. This was all conveniently placed in my lap when I needed something to lift me up out of the hurt and anger.

Was I using her to get back on my feet?

After all, that's the definition of rebound. I met her gaze and blew out my breath.

"Then maybe we should just start as friends," I said.

She stared at me, her lips pouting as she turned over my response. "What if we are incapable of just being friends?"

"By we, you mean me?" I pointed at my chest and raised my eyebrows.

She shrugged a single shoulder and her gaze shifted as the waitress set two glasses of water on the table and I rattled off an order for two steaks, medium rare, Caesar salads and a blooming onion and boneless buffalo wings as appetizers.

"Do you want anything to drink?" I asked after I finished ordering for us.

"This is fine for now." She picked up her water and took a sip, waiting until the waitress was out of range. "I'm capable of ordering for myself," she said.

"I know, but I figured it would save time. Unless you were going to change your mind again?"

She smirked and shook her head. "The fact that's what I was going to order is neither here nor there."

"Okay. From now on, I'll let you order for yourself."

"Thank you," she dipped her head in acknowledgement.

"Now, back to the original conversation. You think I can't keep my hands off you?" I leaned back in the seat and crossed my arms. The smirk was back, and then she slowly shook her head. Well, okay, maybe she was right, but I'd play this game out. I leaned my elbows on the table.

"Game on, baby." I smiled.

The smirk morphed into a grin and that gleam returned to her eyes. I could tell this was going to be a hell of a difficult game to win, but I vowed any time I got the urge to jump her, I'd double-check the underlying reasons, and if Sandy entered my mind in any way, I'd back off.

"So, you were muttering about being behind in your schoolwork last night. What's involved in becoming a doctor, beyond gross anatomy?"

I swear that statement opened Pandora's box. She perked up and started enlightening me about her classes, her challenges, the gross things she's experienced, and while I could almost picture each instance she told me about, the memories didn't do them justice the way she described things. Dinner came and went and when the check was placed on the table, I ignored it, enjoying really laughing again.

I didn't realize how long it had been since I'd laughed with someone instead of laughing out of necessity or sarcasm. It was refreshing as hell.

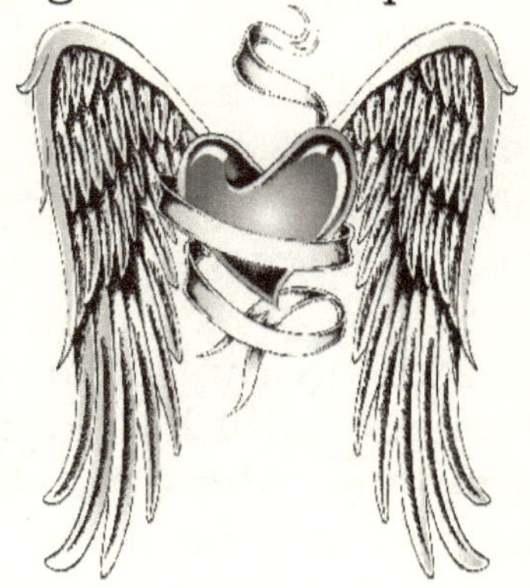

"YOU THINK EVERYTHING AT home is okay?" Valerie asked, as I opened the car door for her.

The light mood fizzled at the reminder of the darkness that shrouded our lives, and I glanced at the dark sky. "No one called, so that's a good sign." I closed the door and scanned the parking lot before I slid into the driver's seat.

Instead of starting the car, I sat contemplating if I could do what Steve did, now that I had the rest of the mojo fused in my blood.

"Try it," she whispered.

I sighed, tempted. "Here isn't the place." I turned the car on and headed home. "I'll try at home." I didn't need to explain why. Just the darkening of my mood was enough.

The question of whether we would ever be able to truly relax and enjoy life settled into my bones. "There's got to be a way to get hell's legions to back the fuck off."

She burst out laughing. "I'm not sure that's possible."

Unfortunately, I agreed with her. I had too much information downloaded into my brain and just couldn't abide by some mutants and monsters that existed. Suddenly, what I really wanted to do with my life overwhelmed me. Instead of sitting by waiting to be attacked, it was my turn to hunt those motherfuckers and put them down.

"I think I should take up hunting." I glanced at Valerie and her eyes widened.

"You can't..."

"Yeah, I can. Damian ran all his life. Look what that got him. It wasn't until he fought back that he won. It wasn't the martyrdom that broke the cycle, it was the attack." I refocused on the road. "I'm better suited to attack than look over my shoulder for the rest of my life."

"Are you out of your fucking mind?" Valerie spouted at my epiphany.

"Seriously, think about it. Everything so far has been defensive maneuvering. It's time to gear up and go on the offensive. Make the monsters run from us for a change."

"Why? Why would you put yourself in that kind of situation?"

I knew she'd had run-ins with some pretty evil assholes, and almost didn't live to tell about it, but she didn't see the beauty in the solution, nor did she get the real reason behind my epiphany. "Someone has to save those kids from a life of running and fear." I refocused on the road in front of me, stopping at the next set of lights. "If Damian isn't prepared to do it, I certainly am."

"Why would you risk your life for someone else's children?"

She really didn't get the scope of what would happen to our world if Lucifer got his hands on Damian's little girl. "Because saving Grace from Lucifer should be a priority for all of us."

"And the boys?"

"Lucifer can't build an army of trinities with them. At least not an army of his offspring, one that he can control. Naomi's at risk too, but I have a feeling if he ever got hold of her, she'd destroy herself before she let him use her for his evil spawn. Besides, there's something special about Grace. Something compelling that makes me want to put my life on the line for her." I bit my lip and turned onto the highway, trying to pinpoint what made the child stand out more than the other two. "It's much more than just the consequences of Lucifer getting his slimy hands on her. It's something deeper." I glanced at Valerie. "You and Naomi have a hint of the same power, albeit much less intense."

"You think it might be our angelic bloodline?"

"Maybe, but I don't feel the same compulsion to protect Damian."

We drove in silence over the Piscataqua River Bridge into Maine. "I'm not sure if it was Damian's innocence or Naomi's specialness, for lack of a more appropriate word, which drove Steve to take a stand with them." *Or if it was just his sense of justice, combined with his untainted moral compass that drove it.*

"Why did you?"

"I wasn't going to let Steve stand alone against what was coming. He's family."

"Damian's my family," she said under her breath.

The last thing I wanted was another Sandy situation, even if it only involved a friend. "I guess that means we'll have to call a truce, then."

Valerie's hand slid over mine and gave a little squeeze and I traded a glance with her and then looked down at my hand covered with hers. She removed her hand, and the absence of her flesh against mine made me sigh. Shutting off access to my thoughts, I stared at the road ahead of me, wondering how in the world I was going to continue playing this game when any time our skin touched it sparked a fire in my soul.

Chapter 17

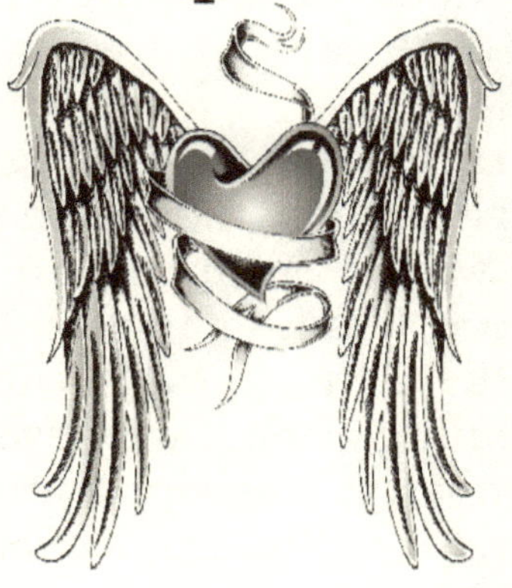

THE HOUSE WAS DARK when we pulled in and Damian's van was gone, along with Steve's truck, and I slowed to a stop in front of Tom's car. Valerie and I exchanged a glance, and she reached for the door. I grabbed her arm.

"Not yet," I said and pulled my phone out of my pocket and dialed. Holding the phone to my ear, I waited, feeling the unease snake into my skin. The call dropped to voicemail, and I ended the call, trying another line.

"Hello?" Raven's Irish brogue came through the line, and I exhaled.

"Hey Raven, where is everyone?"

"You aren't the only one who can decide to grab a fine dinner out on the town," she said over the background noise.

"So, nothing weird happened at the house?"

"No. We let Damian and Naomi experience Wild Willy's while it's slow."

I let out a laugh. "Wild Willy's is never slow."

She laughed too. "I know, right? Anyhow, we're just getting ready to head out."

"Okay, see you in a few."

I folded the phone. "They went out to eat."

"I heard," Valerie said, and we both stepped out of the car.

The chill tonight wasn't as biting as it had been the past few nights, and I hoped that meant spring wasn't far off. I waited on my side of the car for her to join me before heading toward the front door. Halfway down the path, my intuition prickled, and instead of running from whatever stalker had invaded our property, I stopped and mentally told Valerie to stop as well. Taking a moment, I glanced at her and willed the protective bubble around both of us.

We both turned, slowly enough for me to get a whiff of her perfume, the sweet scent grounding me and reminding me I wasn't the only one facing off against whatever it was. When we faced the approaching beast, Valerie threaded her fingers through mine, pulling my attention to our hands and then her eyes. I smiled and gently squeezed her hand, giving her the strength to not scream at the sight before us.

The rabid vampire bear stood on its hind legs and roared. This wasn't a human I could intimidate, nor was it a demon or vampire that had a sense of reason. This was a killing machine, and it was hungry.

I let out a snarling roar of my own, wishing the beast into dust. A swirl of fire engulfed the beast like a destructive tornado until all that was left was fine gray ash.

"Impressive," Valerie said.

The protective field still encompassed us, and I turned toward the house, flipping my phone open again and redialing, keeping Valerie by my side.

"Raven, everyone is with you, right?"

"Yes, we didn't want to leave anyone at home alone."

"Good call." I folded the phone and closed my eyes. "Can you smell them?" I whispered, as my nostrils filled with a foul mixture of brimstone and blood. Her hand tightened on mine, and I opened my eyes, focusing on the downstairs window and the grin that met my gaze.

I pointed. "Come here."

His smile fell into shock as his body stepped into sight.

"What are you doing?"

"Leaving one alive." I glanced at her and when the door opened. I inhaled, putting a duplicate layer of protection around the fiend stepping out of our house. And then I let loose, killing every non-living, pseudo-living and live being from our property line to the ocean breakers at the bottom of the small cliff outside the rock wall. Mini-fire tornados engulfed flesh, leaving the physical property intact as if nothing happened. The only hint of destruction was the gray dust raining to the ground.

The lone demon standing on the stoop stared at me, his face paling, and the first hint of fear gripped his eyes. I released control of his physical form and the protective cocoon around him.

"Let your friends know that I'm coming after them," I said.

He waved his hand and the spark of contact hit our protective barrier. I think he thought he could toss me around like a rag doll, but I was truly supercharged. In kind, I waved my hand toward the gate, tossing him halfway across the lawn. He scrambled to his feet with the front of his jeans now soaked with piss.

"And whoever has the gall to step on this property will end up being roasted alive. Understand?"

The demon nodded, turned tail, and ran out the open gate. I turned back to Valerie with a smirk dancing on my lips.

"You should have torched him as well."

The venom in her tone pulled my gaze to her, and my heart dropped into my stomach. I searched the collective memory banks for some redemption, and there was none. Demon red eyes peered out from Valerie's beautiful face, and I dropped her hand, stepping away.

She had been right next to me all night. And then it occurred to me. She had gotten up and gone to the bathroom. The thing possessing Valerie opened the blazer, showing me the bloodied shirt covering her right side.

"The bitch passed out, and I took over."

I couldn't destroy her, but I could contain her, and I created a force field box around her. One that would stun but not kill the body this prick inhabited.

"Inside," I said, pointing to the opened door. I blocked my thoughts, focusing on the blood, wondering if this shit knew she had the power to heal. My chest hurt as I forced her across to the chair at the head of the table, tying her arms to the hand guards and her legs to the legs of the chair.

I backed into the wall across from her, forcing my breath in and out, keeping the need to scream and tear my hair out at bay.

"I'll let her go if you'll be a dear and let me in," it said.

I covered my mouth, wondering what the hell Damian was going to do. He destroyed the last demon nest without a thought, but this was

Valerie. The girl he saw grow from an infant to the beautiful woman before me.

I regained my composure and stalked right up to her. "Get out of her, you bastard," I growled, but I didn't know the first thing about exorcism. I knew if I could get the shit out of her, then she had more of a chance of survival than anyone on earth. Hell, she might be unconsciously mending as I stood and stared.

The door opened, and the family filtered in, chatting away until the tiger growled. Naomi stepped around the car seat she had the presence of mind to put down before she changed, and Damian's gaping stare met mine.

"She went to the ladies' room right before we left," I said. "I... I didn't know. When I got here, the house was infiltrated, and I destroyed all but one. Well, two." I waved at Valerie. "And after the last one ran with his tail between his legs, this one..." I ran my hand through my hair. "That was when this one made its presence known."

Naomi hissed, pacing a trail blocking Valerie from her children.

I met Tom's gaze and signed for him to take Jen, Steve and Raven upstairs along with the babies. He nodded, and Damian didn't stop them when they disappeared upstairs.

"I couldn't..." I said after everyone else left. Damian's thoughts were sporadic and stinted. He collapsed on the closest ottoman and glanced at the broken lines of salt all over the house. His jaw tightened, and he got up, crossing into the kitchen and disappeared with the salt container. When he came back, he fixed the last three entry points and drew a line across the lowest stair. The last grains fell, and he chucked it across the house, roaring with the same frustration that pounded my muscles.

He grabbed another container and circled the chair. Slamming the container on the table before coming even with me. His shoulder faced me and then his hand shot out, clamping around my throat as he slammed me against the wall. Fury lined his face and Naomi rubbed against his leg, trying to calm the wild beast raging inside him.

I didn't fight back. Whatever he did to me, I deserved it. I was supposed to protect her, and I failed in epic fashion.

His grip loosened and his chin dropped to his chest.

"Don't," I whispered as the power coiled into a tight ball inside him.

"I have to."

"No. You don't. Valerie is still in there. You can't kill her."

He shook his head. "She's not."

"What if it was Naomi," I said and the muscles in his jaw jumped. "There has to be a way."

"She's already dead."

"No. She just passed out, and that gave that thing an opportunity to get in."

"But," he started.

"I don't have everything," I whispered, and his eyes narrowed. His grip loosened more, and he finally dropped his hand as understanding dawned in his eyes. "But I don't know the first thing about exorcism."

"Neither do I," he said.

Naomi continued to pace in agitation.

"You may not know about such things, but I have a potent banishment spell we can try."

Both Damian and I turned toward the stairs where Raven stood, leaning on the railing, her squinting gaze meeting mine and averting Damian's blinding aura.

"Bullshit," Damian said.

Valerie cackled from the seat, her gaze bouncing around the room from the aggravated tiger to Damian and me, and finally landing on Raven. "Your pathetic spells won't work on me," she said, her voice transitioning between demon and Valerie's in an eerie stereo quality.

Raven flipped her hair back with her hand and gave the demon inside Valerie the evil eye. "You'd be surprised at what my spells can achieve," she said and turned, heading upstairs to gather what she needed.

"If this doesn't work, I'm flying her out to the middle of the Atlantic and leaving her there," Damian said.

I couldn't help staring at him, and then I said two words that made Valerie pale.

"Salt water."

Damian nodded, and I closed my eyes, hanging my head. If he did that, hypothermia would kill her before she had a chance to do anything else. There were limitations to the healing power, and while I liked to think what gifts we had made us invincible. The reality was we still had vulnerabilities. A surprise shot to the heart would kill us, same with a bullet in the brain. Our human frailties existed, and there are some people and things that could get the drop on us no matter how diligent we were. Valerie could heal her wound, but the cold water would stop her heart.

I pulled up a chair next to the bound demon and sighed, nodding to Damian.

If what Raven cooked up, didn't work, Valerie would have to be sacrificed.

Chapter 18

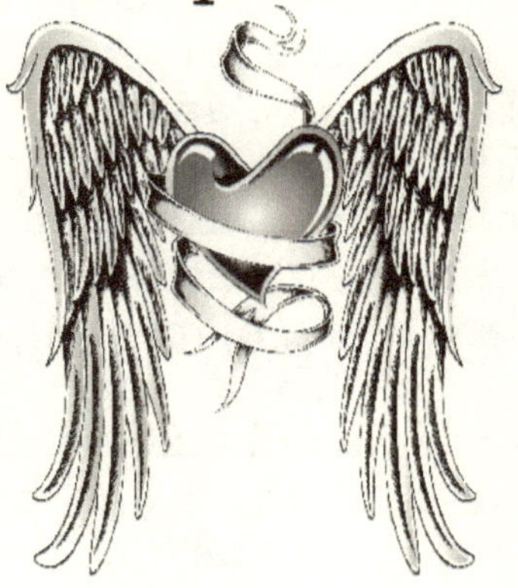

RAVEN CAME DOWN WITH a duffel bag and set it on the table, turning towards Damian and the wild tiger.

"Please, take everyone but Valerie, CJ and me, somewhere while I do this."

A hand banged on the railing, pulling our attention to the stairs. Tom shook his head and pointed to his chest and then the floor, conveying his stance without the flurry of sign language.

"No. I..."

Tom put his palm out, stopping her. I knew that stubborn set of his jaw. There was no way he was leaving her if there was any hint of danger. Besides, his ability to see and even intercept spirits might come in handy.

"Fine," she said and turned back to Damian. "Take Steve, Jen and your wife and kids and go."

"I don't..." Damian started, and Naomi hissed again, this time at him.

He hesitated, and Raven stared him down. "The fewer people here, the better."

There was something more to the warning. She was concerned about the children. About the demon taking over one of their impressionable minds and Damian blanched when Raven's thoughts broadcast her concerns. He nodded, turning and bolting up the stairs. A few minutes later, he came down with Jennifer and Steve, each carrying a car seat and a diaper bag.

"Keep us informed," he said and opened the garage door, letting Naomi take the lead.

Raven waited until the lights disappeared and the gate closed, locking us in. Then she turned, looking between Tom and me. "Are you two ready for a storm?"

Tom nodded without hesitation, and I followed suit. I was ready to brave a hurricane to save Valerie.

Raven started unpacking the duffel bag, setting jewelry, and what looked like fancy paperweights, on the table along with candles and oils and a big sea-salt grinder. She turned and tossed a necklace to me. The black wiccan star reflected in the light, and I raised an eyebrow.

"Just put it on," she said and looked from me to Tom. "Do you have yours on?"

Tom unbuttoned his shirt, showing her the necklace she gave him back in high school for protection against a crazy ghost. It worked back then, and I don't think he'd taken it off since.

I slipped it around my neck and waited while she finished setting up the table. Raven turned and walked into the living room, away from the demon, beckoning to us to follow.

"Block your thoughts," she said.

I consciously put up the wall in my head and nodded, glancing at Tom and then Raven where only static resided. "We're blocked," I said.

She looked at Tom. "The only reason I let you stay is because I may need your special skills."

He started to sign, but she shook her head, stopping him.

"You told me you once put your father's spirit back in his body."

Tom nodded and glanced at me.

"Well, I might need you to do that with Valerie. Okay?"

"Okay," Tom signed.

Raven turned to me. "Do you think your protective shield can repel demon spirits?"

I shrugged. "I don't know."

"Well, let's hope that's the case, because the moment the spirits separate from her physical form and Tom has Valerie's, I'll need you to block anything else from getting to her. Or us, for that matter. She'll still be vulnerable until her spirit is put back in her body. If we fail and the demon gets in there first, she will be lost to us. Understand?"

The layer of doubt that blanketed me must have reflected in my eyes, because Raven's face hardened.

"Understand?" she said, more forcefully this time.

"Yes. I understand," I said. "How do you know this will work?"

"I've seen it done before," she whispered. "But we didn't have the benefit of a ghost whisperer or a psychic shield."

"Did it work?"

She stared at me for a long moment and then shook her head. "No."

"What happened?" I asked, unable to get the details from her mind.

"My father happened," she said and turned away, storming back to the kitchen, leaving Tom and me staring at each other. A chill settled over me and I looked toward the kitchen. Her father was rotting in jail for two consecutive life sentences for the crimes he committed as the Windwalker.

"What do you mean?" I stalked into the kitchen after her, with Tom following.

"We can discuss that later. You know what I expect of you." She turned back to the table and Valerie chuckled. The demon quality of it left me cold.

"I want Val back," I growled at the thing holding her hostage.

"Maybe we can trade?" it said, raising one of her manicured eyebrows.

"As tempting as that sounds, I think I'll see what Raven can do with you first."

A shadow passed over her face and her teeth clenched as she focused on Raven's array of potions and precious rocks on the table.

Raven turned to me. "Can you hold her still for a minute?"

I nodded and wrapped a mental straight jacket around Valerie's body. The demon roared and tried to thrash, but the physical form it inhabited wouldn't budge under my power. The beast within Valerie roared when Raven slipped a bloodstone necklace over her head. The red jewel rested on her chest, right above her heart and the skin under it singed, sending off a waft of steam.

Raven stepped out of the salt ring, visibly shaken by the scorching skin. She glanced at Tom, and he gave her a nod of encouragement. With a deep breath, she arranged four pyramid shaped stones at the north, south, east and west spots inside the circle and stepped back.

In the teak bowl, she mixed salt, some fine black powder and added a drop of green, red, and yellow potions to the mixture. Raven paused and glanced at me, waving me forward. I stepped to her side, and she took my hand. With no explanation, she raked a knife across my palm.

"Squeeze," she said, holding my hand over the mixture.

As bizarre as it sounded, I did what she said and after three drops of blood hit the mixture; she moved my hand away and gave me some sterile gauze. I wrapped the cut and stepped away as she mixed the cocktail and muttered an incantation.

"Mháthair a chara, cruthaitheoir go léir, cabhrú liom banish an Demon as an cailín. Cabhraigh léi a fháil ar ais ar a anam. Dhíbirt an olc as a corp. Cabhraigh léi a fháil ar ais ar a anam. Demon a bheith imithe!"

The mixture bubbled and sizzled, and she turned toward Valerie.

"Repeat after me, boys," Raven said as Valerie started thrashing in the chair. "Spiorad olc saoire an gcomhlacht seo. Demon a bheith imithe!"

Tom and I repeated the foreign chant. "Spiorad olc saoire an gcomhlacht seo. Demon a bheith imithe!"

Raven flung a spoonful of the mix at Valerie and the scream that followed tore at my soul.

When Valerie looked at me and whispered, "Help me." I nearly came undone, but the darkness that flashed over her eyes told me it was a demon trick and not the girl I was willing to lay my life down for.

"Again," Raven ordered and moved to Valerie's side.

We repeated the chant and Raven flung another spoonful at Valerie. This time, the mixture produced scorching welts in her skin, and I stepped towards Raven to stop her from scalding Valerie again, but Tom grabbed my arm and opened his mind. What I saw stopped me. The struggle of souls coming from her writhing form gave me hope and when Raven ordered us to speak the incantation again, I didn't hesitate.

The third time brought forth a wail of pain that made me want to cover my ears. The earth around us rumbled to the point the jars on the counter rattled. The dishes in the cabinets shifted, knocking open cabinet doors and sending plates and glasses crashing to the counter. Even the refrigerator door opened, crashing contents to the floor in a mad swirl.

The fourth time, Tom let go of my arm and stepped forward, grabbing onto something I couldn't see, but his command of "Now" in my head along with the vision of what he held set me in motion and I directed a capsule of protection around the four of us.

Tom took the invisible ghost in his arms and slammed it back into Valerie's body. The melding of spirit to skin arched her back, and she took a deep wheezing breath. Her eyes locked on mine, and she moaned in pain. I glanced at the bloody wound on her side and then back at her.

"Will yourself to heal," I whispered, and her eyes widened and then dropped closed. She sagged in the chair, and I kneeled next to her, untying her arms and legs that had held her in place.

The surrounding air sparked, and Tom glanced up. A black cloud attacked my shield, trying to get back into the body it had been expelled from, and I looked up, using Tom's vision to direct me. With all the anger burning my skin, I sent my wrath toward the demon, willing it to burn. Flames licked the protective bubble and blackened the ceiling and then an explosion rocked the kitchen, blowing the window over the sink open and obliterating the salt line protecting that exit. What was left of the demon spirit fled through that portal, sending a plume of black smoke out into the yard and into the night sky.

Silence fell over us and Tom stepped out of the circle toward the banging window and closed it, replacing the salt line before he turned back to us.

"Is it gone?" I asked, knowing deep down it was, but I didn't trust my instincts right now. They were too colored by my worry for Valerie.

"Yah," Tom said.

I relaxed, sending the protective bubble around the house in case another barrage of creatures attacked.

"Give Steve a call and tell them they can come back," I said to Raven. "And have them call when they get to the gate," I added as I picked Valerie up and brought her to the couch. The scald burns had already faded, and I lifted the hem of her shirt, watching as the stab wound mended.

"It's done. I'll explain when you get home," Raven said into her phone and then pocketed it. She and Tom started the onerous task of cleaning up the mess the demon created.

"Why my blood?" I asked, and Raven turned toward me.

"Only love's blood works," she said and offered me a fleeting smile before continuing to sweep up the glass covering the kitchen floor.

I stared at the blood-soaked bandage around my hand and then at Valerie. I knew I'd die for her, but love? Really? The rational side of my brain scoffed, and I wiped the hair out of her face, ignoring the pounding of my heart and the relief saturating my muscles. Instead, I retrieved a wet washcloth and gently began wiping the blood from her now unmarred side.

Her eyes fluttered open, and she met my gaze.

"Hey," I whispered, and continued cleaning the evidence from her skin.

She pressed her lips together and covered her mouth with the back of her hand. Tears immediately sprang from her eyes, and she focused on the ceiling. Her entire form shook, and I dropped the cloth and pulled her into my arms. She clung to me, trembling and sobbing at the horrors she experienced during the demon possession.

"I killed..." she whispered in my ear.

"No, you didn't," I said, pulling away and wiping her face.

"The waitress. The one who stabbed me. I... I..." she trailed off and swallowed. "I saw everything," she added. "Oh, God, Chris. If you had tried that thing in the car..." she shuddered. "I was so terrified you were going to and kept screaming for you not to. If you had, it would have gotten you. It would have stolen your body."

I smiled and smoothed her hair back. "Well, then, it's a good thing I didn't try now, isn't it?"

Her chin quivered, and she nodded, throwing her arms around me, and burying her face in my neck. I rubbed her back and cooed "shhh" as she started crying again. The phone rang and Tom picked it up, muttering hello in his unintelligible way. I traded a glance with him, and he gave the thumbs up. Concentrating, I opened a gate in my protective barrier until I heard the car pull into the garage and then the opening slammed closed.

Damian charged in the house with Naomi running after him in human form. His gaze jumped from the destroyed kitchen to the couch where I held Valerie and he stopped. Naomi bumped into him with one of the boy's car seat on her arm.

Steve and Jennifer stepped into the house behind them and closed the garage door. The babies were relinquished to their parents and Jennifer stared at the damage, crossing to the kitchen with her mouth drawn in a frown. I couldn't help but laugh. Jennifer and the kitchen were fleeting connections. She couldn't cook worth a damn, and I would have expected Steve to be more distraught.

"What..." Jennifer said and waved toward the glass speckled counters and the swept piles of debris.

"It could have been worse," I said. "The demon could have blown up your stove."

Jennifer's head snapped in my direction. As soon as my words sank in, her face transformed into a smile, followed by a small giggling laugh. Being privy to the joke, Steve, Tom and Raven joined her.

Yeah, leave it to me to crack up the crowd.

Damian was not at all amused, but I guess he wouldn't be. He never had to endure anything Jennifer cooked. Valerie pulled away from my chest and wiped her face before turning toward him.

"You're really okay?" he asked, taking a tentative step towards us.

"Yes. Raven has quite the talent for banishing demons," she said.

"Oh, that reminds me," Raven said and propped the broom against the wall. She rifled through the duffel bag, pulling out four more pendants. She crossed, handing one to each of the adults, and then her gaze fell on the children.

"I think I might actually have something to protect them as well," she said and marched back to her bag of tricks. She dug around in the bag and pulled a little pouch out.

We all watched as she pulled out half a dozen crocheted bracelets with gems embedded in the designs. She peeled off three of the smallest ones and crossed to the babies, tying the bracelet on each ankle for a loose fit that wouldn't slide off.

"That will do for a while," she said, looking up at us.

"What are these?" Naomi asked, turning her pendant over.

"They're tourmaline pendants. They'll protect you from evil spirits," Raven said and crossed back to the kitchen. Instead of grabbing the broom, she went to the table and started packing up her bag of tricks.

"They work," Tom signed.

He knew firsthand, but a ghost was much different from a demon and I wasn't sure it would protect us from a demon attack the way it did with Tom and his crazy ghost.

"I know they work on ghosts, but..."

Raven snapped her gaze to mine and stopped packing. "It wards off evil."

"So, I can take down the protective barrier?" I waved towards the roof and her gaze jumped from me to the outside and back. Hesitation colored her face, but eventually she nodded.

"If you want to test the theory, be my guest."

I most certainly did not want to put my family at risk, so I left the barrier in place.

Damian studied his pendant and then let it drop to his chest. "I've seen a couple of these along my travels, but it does nothing to deter a hungry vampire," he said, bringing the point home. "I'm not sure about demons," he added with a shrug.

Raven waved toward Valerie. "It certainly helped her," she said and zipped up her bag, lugging it back upstairs.

I couldn't argue with that, although I think it was the entire ritual that helped, not just the necklace. Valerie turned toward me, and her gaze dropped to my hand.

"I think this was the magic ingredient," she whispered and brought my palm to her lips.

I clamped my teeth together, offering a tight smile as the healing pain took hold.

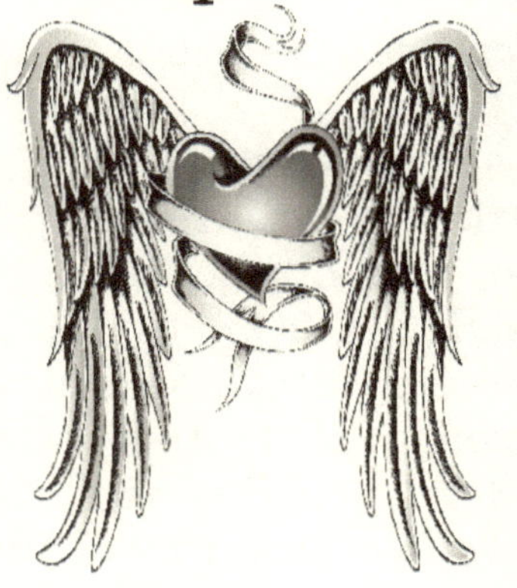

THE HOUSE WAS QUIET, and I glanced at the clock on the wall. It was only three in the morning and I was exhausted. Despite that, I forced my eyes to remain open and the force field outside to stay intact. It was only a few more hours until dawn and then I could let my guard down.

The stair creaked, and I rolled onto my side, meeting Valerie's gaze.

"I couldn't sleep," she said.

I wished that was my problem. I was having a hard time staying awake. I just sent a smile in her direction instead of voicing my thoughts.

"Are you okay?" I sat up as she approached, making space for her on the couch.

"Not really." She plunked down next to me and wrapped her arms around my arm, using my shoulder as a headrest. "Thank you."

"Why are you thanking me?"

"Because if you hadn't convinced Damian to give Raven's mojo a try, I'd be dead right now."

I remained silent and covered her hand with mine. "I didn't do it for you," I said after a few minutes of soul searching. "It was a matter of self-preservation."

She lifted her head and looked at me. "What do you mean?"

I let out a small laugh. "I was responsible for that demon getting to you. If I didn't try, and I had let Damian take you out to sea…" I pulled out of her grip and slid out from under the covers. The moonlight danced on the water outside and I stared at the hypnotizing patters the waves made before continuing. "If I let you die without trying to save you, I would have lost faith in winning this war."

She joined me at the window, wrapping her arms around my waist from behind. "You wouldn't have given up," she whispered in my ear.

I focused on the reflection in the window, on her calico eyes. She didn't know how close to the edge I really was. "Babe, I'm a disaster away from falling apart."

The admission raked its weak nails across my skin, leaving a gradual burn that turned in my stomach. I didn't like being on the edge. It was not a comfortable place for me and my volatile gifts.

She reached out, cupping my cheek, and turned my head towards her. I met her gaze and shifted to face her. "No, you're not," she said and pulled me to her lips before I could correct her.

Time stopped, and I think I stopped breathing with it. Her kiss captivated me like nothing else ever had. Her hands slid from around my neck, down my chest, and around my waist. Just the feel of her fingertips on my skin lit a fire inside me and the t-shirt she wore wasn't enough to save her from the need ripping through me.

It was animalistic and fierce, and I tore the fabric from her body in a fit of uncontrollable lust. I maneuvered her past the couch and up the stairs, our lips only parting in order to take a breath. Before I knew it, I was on top of her on my bed with my hands caressing her breasts and my mouth savoring her hard nipples. She clutched a fistful of my hair and pulled me back to her lips.

I shifted and traced the lines of her stomach down to her underwear, smiling at the sudden appearance of goose bumps all over her flesh. The thin fabric between her legs was damp, and I broke the kiss, moving down her body, teasing her with my tongue.

Valerie made a sweet noise of surrender when I pressed my mouth to her underwear, blowing a breath through the fabric. I didn't wait for acknowledgement, instead; I ripped the underwear from her body and tossed it to the floor.

She followed the progression of the ruined fabric and then looked at me. "I just bought those," she whispered.

"So?" I said and pushed her thighs apart. The moment my tongue parted her, I think all her thoughts and retorts disappeared. She sighed and twirled a lock of my hair in her fingers, enjoying the spoils of my mouth. I gently slid my finger inside her, and she moaned softly, further fueling the fire inside me.

I tapped into her mind, reading the things that she liked and those that were 'eh'. She wanted more, more of me, and I followed her desires, bringing her over the brink more than once before I worked my way back up to her mouth.

The urge to tear off my shorts and fuck the daylights out of her took hold, but I resisted. Valerie shifted, pushing me onto my back and then she broke the kiss, traveling down my body with her lips, teasing me in a way I never knew existed.

She pulled my shorts to my knees, and I propped up on my elbows. "Val," I warned, and then her mouth swallowed the tip of my cock and I forgot all about my warning. Instead, I watched her suck and lick and swallow me whole. She was fucking fantastic.

She shifted again, and I smiled when she planted her knees on either side of my head. She might be a virgin, but damned if she didn't know the art of oral sex. I pulled her toward me and fucked her with my tongue and fingers, making her moan around my cock. She came again and again, and I forced myself to hold off, to prolong the heaven that was her mouth. Each stroke of her lips brought me closer to my climax and, finally, I let go.

My entire body went rigid with the power of it, and I sucked her harder, groaning against her soaking pussy. Valerie didn't pull away; instead, she swallowed, gently sucking until I said okay.

She shuffled into the crook of my arm, and we stared at the ceiling, unable to speak. Hell, I have no idea how she could move, because I certainly couldn't right now.

"That was fucking brilliant," she whispered.

I couldn't help it. I laughed. "Brilliant?" I turned my head toward her.

She grinned. "Fucking brilliant."

I had never been referred to as fucking brilliant in bed, but then again, I really only had Sandy as a reference and nothing we ever did compared to this.

"You were fucking brilliant," I smiled.

"I'm not sure about that." Her cheeks turned crimson, almost glowing in the darkness.

"This surpasses anything I've experienced to date. You were fucking brilliant." I leaned towards her and grabbed a kiss.

"So, I'm better than a houseful of demons?" she teased.

"Worlds," I said. "Even without the bondage."

She covered the laughter with her hand, stifling the sound. I chuckled softly, wondering just how mind blowing that would be. The only thing more satisfying than what I just experienced would be making love to the girl. My smile faltered, and I stared at the ceiling again as the thoughts stirred me back to life.

I started to slide out from under her before I did something she didn't want, and she pushed me back down.

"Don't go."

"Val, hon, if I stay, I'm going to pin you to this bed and..." I inhaled and went to sit up. This time, she pushed me down and swung her leg over me, coming up into a straddle position. I stared into her eyes, the swirling pattern as hypnotizing as the ocean's moon dance.

"Val," I said, again, as her hips slowly swirled, grinding me back to life. "Ah, fuck, Val," I whispered and pulled her to my lips.

The sweetness of sliding inside her overwhelmed me and she winced, stiffening for a moment before settling down on top of me. She met my gaze and offered a forced smile and I put my hands on her thighs, holding her in place.

"Relax," I said, and little by little, she did.

She started with slow hip grinding circles, and I moved my thumb to her clit, circling lightly enough for her to forget the pain. I let her set the pace, keeping eye contact with her through it all, and prayed she wouldn't regret this in the morning light.

She smiled down at me, rolling her hips in circles in time with my thumb.

"You like that?" I asked, raising an eyebrow.

"Yes." The breathless quality of her voice reached into my heart, taking another piece of it with her.

Valerie started sliding herself up and down my shaft in concert with her hip twirls, and I thought I had died and gone to heaven. She was hot and wet and so fucking tight. I wanted to flip over and take control, but I didn't want to hurt her again, and I was sure my control meant complete loss of such, so I let her get off with the slow ride.

I gripped her hips, moving her a little faster, until I felt the buildup start. She arched into me, covering her own moan with her hand as she contracted, squeezing the cum right out of me. She shuddered, twirled her hips a couple of more times and collapsed on top of me while my body trembled with aftershocks.

"Holy Christ," she whispered in my ear, and I wrapped my arms around her, planting a kiss on her cheek.

"Complete and utter mind fuck," I said, and she pushed away, meeting my gaze.

She didn't understand what I meant, and the hurt in her eyes made me sigh.

"I'm now sure," I said.

"About what?"

"You are *not* a rebound."

Her head tilted.

"Everything before you was."

Her hands fluttered to her mouth and her eyes filled with tears. Valerie's mind was open enough for me to know they weren't tears of sadness. I'd touched her in a way she had never felt before.

So, we were pretty much even in that respect.

Chapter 20

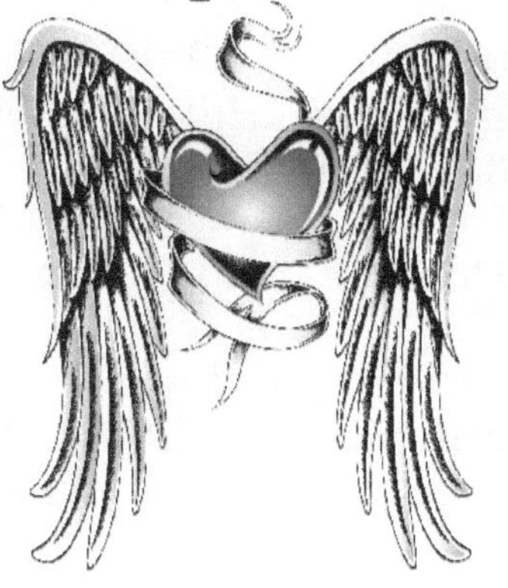

SUNSHINE STREAKED THROUGH THE room, and I blinked, wiping the sleep from my eyes, and looked down at the head of brown hair resting on my chest. I turned toward the clock and stared at the numbers as they changed from 12:59 to 1:00.

"Shit," I whispered and tried to shuffle out from under her, but my arm was dead weight, sound asleep underneath Valerie. "Val," I whispered, and she stirred, lifting her head. She stared at me and then at us, still naked and entwined and then back at me, with arched eyebrows.

"Yeah, it wasn't a dream." I grinned.

"Holy crap." She moved her gaze to the clock. I sensed the panic and when her gaze came back to mine, it was there. Thoughts of what Damian would do surfaced in her mind and then on the heels of that. She looked down at me and covered her mouth.

My smile faded. We didn't use protection. It never even entered my mind last night; or hers, for that matter. I blinked and slammed my head back into the pillow. Pregnancy was a complication neither of us needed right now.

"I'm sorry." I tucked the hair behind her ear.

"It's not entirely your fault. I didn't think of it either." She dropped her head to my chest.

"Still think it was fucking brilliant?"

She looked up at me and grinned. "A complete mind fuck."

I chuckled, and she did too.

"Utterly impractical of both of us." Dimples appeared in her cheeks. "Who would have thought?"

"Raven, actually," I said, thinking about the blood sacrifice needed for the spell. "She knew I loved you before I did."

Valerie pulled the sheets around us before refocusing on me. "How?"

"Beats the shit out of me, but she said only love's blood made the spell work."

"Sounds like a fairy tale," she scoffed and rolled her eyes.

"Yes, it does," I said, and I really didn't mind as long as the fairy tale had a happy ending.

Her brow creased. "That's sappy as hell," she said to my train of thought.

"Come on. And you don't want a happy ending?" I prodded.

She stared at me and then moved her gaze to the window and the bright sky beyond. "I didn't think I was destined for it, with all that's happened." When she brought her gaze back to mine, doubt laced them.

"And now?"

"I'm still afraid of the big bad wolf." She offered a hint of a smile. "We need to get moving." She slid off me, crossing to the bags on the floor.

I stared at her beautiful form and sighed as she pulled on a bathrobe and collected her clothing and headed toward the bathroom, leaving me alone with my thoughts.

I rolled onto my side, squeezing my fist open and closed as pins and needles struck. I hated the feeling of a limb coming back to life. and gritted my teeth, shaking the feeling back into my arm. I rolled out of bed and grabbed a pair of clean underwear and jeans, sliding both on before straightening out the bed and headed downstairs.

Steve sat in his chair with the paper again, but this time, he folded the corner over and stared at me. I didn't need to read minds to get that he was not pleased with me. Damian stepped into the kitchen from the living room with a baby in his arms. The look on his face was ten times more damning than Steve's.

"We're both adults," I said, clamping down on the urge to say she started it. I put my hand out to stop whatever wrath the ex-vampire was planning on sending my way.

Raven sat at the table opposite Naomi, feeding the other two children. Both women wore the same "I told you so" shit-eating grins.

"Under my roof?" Steve said, and I shot a glare in his direction. It was enough to shut him up, but he folded the paper and set it down on the table next to her shredded night shirt. He picked it up and held it out to me.

I stared at the ripped fabric and uttered a laugh. "Oops," I said and shrugged. Tom snorted laughter from the loveseat, looking up from the book he was reading, and gave me a silent high five.

"You..." Damian began through a set of clamped teeth.

"He loves her," Raven said, announcing my secret to the world and diffusing a potentially explosive situation. Well, the only world of people that counted, anyway.

I shifted and looked at the floor, sliding my gaze to hers, and then rolled my eyes and crossed into the kitchen. I figured I was safe from Damian's wrath while he held a baby in his arms.

"You're not out of the doghouse yet," he whispered as I walked past and I stopped, turning on him.

"We can take it outside again if you'd like," I said, leveling a glare at him. "Because that worked out so well for you before."

His jaw tightened, and he turned, stomping back into the living room. I smiled and grabbed a glass of orange juice, thinking about how I would feel had the tables been turned. My smile faded and because the jackass meant a lot to Valerie, I headed into the living room and took a seat opposite Damian.

"When did you know you loved Naomi?" I asked, and he glared at me. I knew the answer, but I wanted him to say it.

"When I bit her," he finally said.

"So pretty much at first taste."

His lips pressed into a thin line, and his gaze hardened. "It wasn't the same as seducing a virgin," he growled.

"Oh?" My eyebrows shot up, and I leaned forward. "Wasn't she a virgin when you swept her away?" I didn't think it was possible for the man to get redder, but his face transitioned to the beet color of fury, and I felt the waves wash over me. "Besides, *I* didn't just take her virginity in the heat of the moment." I tilted my head, making my point.

"That still doesn't make it right. You took advantage..." he trailed off, glaring at me a second before his gaze moved to the entry.

Valerie stood with her arms crossed, sending her own glare. But this time it wasn't aimed at me.

"He really didn't have a choice in the matter," she said and stepped into the room.

It wasn't entirely true; I probably could have stopped if I wanted to.

She shot her loaded gaze in my direction, raising her eyebrows in jest, to my train of thought. I offered a one shoulder shrug and then she shot her dagger-like eyes back to Damian. "So, if you're going to go on one of your tirades, it better damned well be directed at me, not him."

Holy hotness, she was a fireball, and I couldn't help but smile and be thankful her fury wasn't aimed at me.

"Besides, he was the one who bet on me. You were ready to write me off."

Ah, the real reason for her wrath, and I leaned back in my chair watching the show unfold, wondering if it was going to be a comedy or tragedy.

My analogy drew a smirk on Damian's face, and he slid his gaze to me. The redness in his face had tempered a bit, and he pulled the bottle from the baby's mouth, propping him on his shoulder for a burp before meeting Valerie's stark stare again.

"You have to understand..." he started.

Colossal mistake.

"I don't have to understand a fucking thing," she growled. "I've known you all my life, and you gave up. I've only known him for what, three days? Three days and he had enough faith to believe saving me was possible."

"Faith has nothing to do with it. He wanted to get you into bed. That's it."

"Bullshit!" she yelled. "He chose to save me. You didn't. What would Michael think of that?"

Damian winced. She nailed a nerve, and he looked down at the angel's namesake with an expression full of regret.

"Or did you just choose to give up on him, too?" she asked, her fury pulling the low blow.

"Wait a minute, Val, that's not fair," I piped in. "I was there. What Michael and Gabriel did was to save Naomi and the babies regardless of the consequences."

"You don't need to defend me," Damian said.

I glanced at him. "You didn't kill them. You didn't kill my father, either. They made the choice. As much as we'd like to take the blame, it was their choice."

"Yes. But she's right. I gave up on her and you didn't. It was my choice, and I chose my children."

His words were like a blow in Valerie's midsection, and she reached for the wall. A blend of aggravation and understanding ran through her as her gaze moved from him to his child.

"I would have made the same choice if it had been Naomi," he said, and her gaze jumped back to his. "I didn't believe banishment spells worked and you're damned lucky it did because I would have dropped you in the middle of the Atlantic otherwise." His mouth curled into a frown. "I would have hated myself forever, but I would have done it."

Her mouth dropped open and her eyes glazed over with tears.

"You'll understand someday," he said and stood, leaving us alone in the living room.

Her horrified gaze snapped to me, and I stood, crossing and taking her in my arms. Her last vestige of family ties unraveled, and she hugged me tightly, retreating into herself and she rebuilt the wall I broke down last night.

"Please, don't shut me out," I whispered, feeling her pull away.

She tilted her head up, meeting my gaze.

"How can I trust anyone?"

I smoothed her hair back and gazed into her eyes. When I kissed her, I opened up my mind to her. Everything I kept locked in the dark corners, things that didn't transfer with my memories. My fears, the hurt, the betrayals, the loneliness, everything that molded me into the man I was. Things I didn't even share with Tom. I shared with her and when the kiss broke, she stared at me.

"Colossal mind fuck," she whispered.

I smiled and shrugged. "Now you know me better than anyone on earth, better than even my brother."

She cupped my cheek and gave me a small peck on the lips, knowing just how much I opened up, but her eyes still held doubt.

"What do I need to do?" I asked, my smile fading at the blockade building between us.

"I don't know," she said and pulled out of my arms.

I stared after her as she walked back inside the house with the rest of the family. Instead of following, I went upstairs and jumped in the shower to wash off the irritation building under my skin. It wasn't easy for me to open up, either, and to get so brutally shot down, just fed into my insecurities. And I hated I had insecurities to begin with.

The shift of air interrupted my destructive train of thought.

"I didn't shoot you down," Valerie said.

"Then what was that?" I gestured toward the main part of the house.

"That was me freaking out." She leaned against the wall. "It doesn't happen often." A dimple appeared in her cheek. "But since I've met you, I've had my fair share of freak outs."

I finished rinsing my body and turned the water off, reaching for a towel before addressing her comment. "I thought you didn't freak out." It wasn't a question, just an open-ended statement.

"You unhinge me," she said, and I couldn't help but laugh. "Stop laughing at me," she snipped and turned toward the door.

I grabbed her arm. "Then we're even," I said, and she spun toward me. I cornered her against the door. "Unhinged is as good a word as anything to describe what I'm like around you." I stepped closer. "I have a bitch of a time forming a coherent thought and become a bumbling fool when I'm near you. I'm a fucking genius for god's sake, and yet, with you, I feel like I have an I.Q. of an infant." I was mad now.

"Calm down," she said and put her palms on my chest. Just her touch shut my brain down for a moment and I stepped back, giving us both some breathing room so I could get my thoughts together from jumble land.

"I opened up to you, and you shut down on me."

"I'm not very good at this," she said.

"No shit." I couldn't help the sarcasm. It was my favorite default, and she knew it.

Her arms crossed and her stormy eyes darkened. "You aren't exactly the smoothest, either."

I laughed and took another step back. I knew it was a way to psychologically put distance between us, and her eyes narrowed. She called it before the words formed and I put my hands up in surrender.

"You started the barricade. I'll finish it because I don't want to be crushed beyond recognition."

She stepped toward me, and I steeled myself against the need to give in. She froze and drew her hand back slowly.

"You could destroy me," I said, meeting her gaze, not really understanding how it could be such a solid fact with so little time invested. I didn't want this type of dependency. I guess mind fuck was really an appropriate term to put to this overwhelming certainty.

Valerie let a nervous laugh escape, but her eyes didn't break away from mine. Instead, she crossed the distance, blocking me in. I flinched when she went to touch me, knowing I'd lose my ability to distance myself if her skin connected to mine.

The closer she got, the more the storm colors in her eyes swirled, and when her hands connected with my chest, I lost control of my reserve.

"Don't do this if you have no intention of following through," I whispered, and she pressed the rest of her body against me, taking full advantage of my weakness. Her hand threaded through my hair, and she pulled me to her lips.

A shadow passed over my vision and I closed my eyes, drinking in her vulnerabilities, her fears, her sorrow and uncertainties. She opened everything to me, including her deadly fear of losing me to my past or worse, to the devil. When the kiss broke, I opened my eyes, meeting hers and I let a small smile of understanding form.

I walked some of the same pathways, had the same fears, and only God knew why we were thrown together, but I took a moment to say thank you. He could have let me wander like a lost nomad, but he delivered her to my door, gift wrapped in sass and strength.

I glanced up at our surroundings and then back down at her. "We have to stop meeting in the bathroom."

She grinned. "I like having you in nothing but a towel. It makes you vulnerable. And you're adorable when you're vulnerable."

Just what a guy wants to hear. I ran my hand through my wet hair and chuckled. "I thought you just liked the view."

"Well, that, too," she said, and I sidestepped around her, heading to the bedroom for a change of clothes. She followed, closing the door behind her. At first, I thought she was going to make another move on me, but she took a seat at my desk and stared out the window instead.

"What's up?" I asked after I had a pair of jeans on. I pulled a flannel shirt on and started buttoning it before I glanced at her contemplative profile.

She turned away from the window, meeting my gaze. "How's this going to work?"

I shrugged. "How's what going to work?"

"Us. This." She pointed at her chest, then me. "I've still got another year of med school and then two years in rotations, followed by residency. It's going to be a few years before I get any kind of break."

"Would you consider something closer?" I asked. I really didn't want to leave my family high and dry right now, nor did I want to leave her alone, even with her home as secure as Fort Knox. She still had to go out, no matter where she was. My gaze dropped to the necklace Raven had given her and then back to her eyes.

"Where?" she finally said, not wanting to shoot my ideas down after the last twenty minutes of strife we conquered.

"How about somewhere in Boston? That's closer than Farmington."

She scoffed at me. "What? Like Harvard?"

"It is the number one medical school in the country." I raised my eyebrows.

"I can't afford that," she said.

I pressed my lips together, suppressing the smile. "I can."

"I don't want your money," she said and stood up.

"Would you like a medical degree from Harvard?" I asked, keeping my voice soft and reasonable. And her eyes sparked with interest.

"I can't afford it, so it's not an option."

"Can you get into Harvard?" I purposely kept using the name of the school and every time I did, I saw the inclination to keep me pushing.

"Of course I can," she snapped, her hands finding her hips. "I may not be a fucking genius, but I'm damned smart."

"I never said you weren't," I smiled. "And you damned well know you want a degree from the best school in the country." I stepped closer. "Transfer and I'll foot the bill just to have you closer."

She opened her mouth to say no, but closed it just as quickly, studying me. "If I say no, you'll come to Connecticut with me, right?"

The conflict between my family and her brewed inside me, but I nodded, anyway. If that's what she insisted on, I'd follow her. After all, I was just tinkering and could do that anywhere. Same with teaching self-defense. It didn't tie me to a place like the path to what she wanted to do.

"Harvard?" she asked after a few minutes of silence.

"If that's what you want."

"What about my house?"

I shrugged and looked at the ceiling. "This is legally mine now that I'm over twenty-one."

"What about Tom?"

"He's got a place in New Hampshire and an option to take the house across town once the lease runs out."

"And Steve and Jen?"

"They've got a place in New Hampshire and New York."

She got quiet, studying me in a way that made me wonder what was churning behind those beautiful eyes.

I loved this quaint little town. It was home, and I really didn't want to leave it behind. It was all I had left of my parents. I waited for her to decide, and then she nodded.

"Connecticut is probably not the best place for either of us to be right now," she said, and her eyes darkened. "Besides, my house is one of Lucifer's prime targets, so a change would probably be in order."

"So, Harvard?" I asked.

"I guess I can at least apply," she conceded. "But when things blow over here, I will need to take a ride to pick up some things."

"That's no problem. I'd really like to see Michael's artwork."

Her smile faded. "Didn't Damian booby trap the basement?"

I grinned. "I'm a fucking genius, remember?" Damian was borderline genius, but I could get around his computer programming as easily as an adult could snatch a piece of candy from a child.

She laughed and turned toward the laptop on my desk. "Do you mind?"

"Not at all," I said and turned it on, typing the passcode in and relinquishing the computer to her.

I went to leave when a familiar voice came through the speakers.

My blood chilled, and I kept my back to the Skype screen that was set to automatically come up when she called.

"Who the hell are you?" Sandy said.

Valerie didn't speak, she just got up and gave me a sideways glance as she passed, leaving me alone with the video screen of my ex.

"Val, you don't have to leave," I said, and she turned at the door, meeting my gaze. The fear present in her eyes shut down my voice. She gave me the slightest of nods before disappearing down the hallway. The hurt in her eyes haunted me and set my fury switch on high.

"Chris, who was that?"

"None of your fucking business," I said, still refusing to turn. I stared at the empty hallway and my heart pounded in my chest.

"I'm sorry, Chris. I fucked up."

My hands clenched into fists, and I glared over my shoulder. Her hazel irises were surrounded by red lines, like she had been crying. It dug under my skin, but whatever I may have felt for the girl died the moment that door opened.

"You're too late for apologies."

"Please…"

"No. I didn't fuck around on you with the first girl who threw herself my way, and honey, I had a lot of girls propositioning me over the years. But you, you jump into bed with the first guy that turns on the charm just to get in your pants. Was he the first one or just one of many?" The anger blew wide open, and I knew the dig was wrong, but I couldn't help it.

I shouldn't be reacting like this, but the callous way she let me loose really burned my ego. The fact

I had Valerie didn't make a difference where Sandy's shitty treatment was concerned. I leaned over, planting my fists on the desk. The fury encompassing me was a massive beast, and I almost lost control of it until a hand landed on my shoulder.

I looked at the hand's owner and my fury reined in. Valerie's touch tempered the wild beast, and I refocused on Sandy.

"You're right, you fucked things up beyond the ability to ever fix."

Tears welled up in her eyes.

"I was wrong," she whispered, and then the screen tilted, widening the shot.

I took an involuntary step back, bumping into Valerie. A sick understanding swept through my gut as I stared at her possessed boyfriend and the knife he held to her throat. Three days ago, I would have been on my knees begging for her life, but now, I just stared at her, with a total sense of loss raking my skin.

"That's not your boyfriend," I said softly, and a crease appeared between her eyes. "I mean it was, but now he's possessed by one of hell's demons."

"He's right," Josh whispered in her ear, his red eyes shined in the camera. "And he's going to either trade his soul for you or watch you die."

Sandy paled, and her eyes widened. As much as she'd hurt me, she really didn't deserve to die for it. The anger flooded back into my skin, and I shook my head.

"My soul is not a bargaining chip," I said and concentrated, opening my hand and envisioning it wedged between the knife and her throat.

Tears sprang to Sandy's eyes, and she shook as fear blazed through her slight form.

"Say goodbye," the demon said, and the knife sliced flesh.

Pain and anger fueled me, and I took a step right into her room. Both their eyes widened, and I pushed out a blast of power along with the roar of fury that escaped my lips. Josh, and the demon possessing him, exploded. The sound of it was wet and vile, followed by the sound of metal on tile as the knife hit the ground.

I stared at Sandy's shocked gaze and stepped back into my room, blinking at her image on the screen and the blood-soaked room behind her. She shook in the seat, just staring at me. I dropped my gaze to my hand and the gash splitting the skin to the bone. Throbbing pain resonated up my arm, and I moved my gaze back to Sandy.

"Are you okay?" I asked.

She shook her head, on the verge of hysteria. "Did you say demon?" she asked, her voice shaking as much as her body.

"Yes." I glanced at Valerie. "Think you can go get me one of Raven's stone necklaces?" I asked her and she nodded and left the room. I focused back on Sandy. "A lot has happened in the last couple of weeks." I refrained from saying she'd know what was going on had she not been fucking that asshole when I came by.

She let out a high-pitched laugh and her gaze dropped to the knife.

"He... he," she gulped and brought her gaze back to mine.

I raised my hand into view, and she stared at the ugly gash. Her chin trembled, and tears snaked down her cheeks. Valerie stepped to my side and handed me a necklace with one of the smaller black pendants.

I took it in my good hand and met her gaze. The hurt there burned in the pit of my stomach. "Watch my back, okay?" I asked, and she nodded without speaking. I refocused on the monitor and stepped forward.

This time, the tingling sensation of the transition overtook me, and I stepped into her dorm room, opposite the desk she sat at. Her gaze bounced from the monitor to me, and I moved around the desk to her side, unclasping the necklace in my hand and putting it on her. When she moved to throw her arms around my neck, I caught them and shook my head, pushing her gently back into the chair.

"I was serious before. It's over and there's no backtracking. I just want to make sure you're safe," I said and let go of her arms. My blood stained her forearm, and she looked at the blotch and then my hand.

"You really saved my life," she said, and I stood, stepping back to the front of the desk.

"Yeah," I said and let the transition take hold.

Sandy stared at me on the monitor and her gaze dropped to her arm and then the necklace before returning to mine.

"Why?" she asked as the shakes quelled.

"Because no matter how angry I am at you, you don't deserve to die."

She blinked and made the mistake of looking over her shoulder. "Oh, god," she gasped, and her hand shot over her mouth, but not quickly enough to stop the flow of vomit.

"Sorry about the mess," I said, and she gagged and spit before looking back at me. "Wear the necklace. It'll keep you safe," I added as her gaze transitioned from horror to panic.

"How am I supposed to explain this?" she asked, pointing her thumb over her shoulder.

I looked at the dripping walls and shrugged. "Freak accident?"

She burst out laughing, but it was that 'I've gone over the edge' laugh that would transition to a scream any second.

"I gotta go. I need my hand fixed," I said, and she nodded, still laughing that edgy laugh. I shut down the session before she started screaming and turned toward Valerie.

"Are you okay?" My concern for her was greater than it had been for Sandy.

"Yes. Are you?" she asked, and I knew damned well she didn't mean my hand.

"Honestly, I'm numb right now." I wasn't sure when my actions would catch up to me, but right now I was still riding the adrenaline high that kept real feelings at bay.

She reached down and took my wounded hand. "Have you ever done this before?"

I just raised an eyebrow. She had the memories; she knew this was the first time I'd put myself between a blade and someone I cared about. Whether or not I wanted to admit it, I cared about what happened to Sandy. It was in my nature to protect those close to me, and Sandy had been one of those people for fifteen years.

"Okay, stupid question," she said and pulled my palm to her lips.

Pain magnified. "Oh, fuck, that hurts," I whispered.

She smiled, wiping the blood stain from her lips. "Not numb anymore, eh?"

I rolled my eyes and squeezed my hand, pressing it to my chest. "At least I don't pass out from the fucking pain," I snapped and turned away, trying not to double over. A deep wound hurt worse than broken bone and I forced my breath into shallow pants, repeating the word fuck with every exhale. The springs on my bed creaked, and I glanced over at Valerie.

She seemed to be highly amused by my pain.

"What are you smiling at," I hissed.

"You." She crossed her arms. "The ultimate hero acting like a major wuss."

"It fucking hurts," I growled.

"I'm sure, but you're dancing around like a kid having a tantrum."

"No, I'm not," I said and straightened. Okay, maybe I had been, but in my defense the pain made me nutty. I've had broken bones mended along with scrapes and bruises, but never to-the-bone slices before. It was more than just unpleasant, and I glanced at her side and then back to her eyes. No wonder she passed out cold.

The pain abated, replaced by that weird pins and needles sensation that drove me equally insane. I started flexing and squeezing my hand until it passed, and then I took a seat next to her, staring at my closed monitor.

With the numbness gone, the full impact of everything I'd done hit and I dropped my chin to my chest. "Oh, man," I whispered just as the shakes took hold and my stomach started that slow roll that sent me running. I made it in time, spilling the contents of my stomach into the toilet bowl.

Valerie kneeled next to me and rubbed my back. I spit, flushed, and then met her gaze.

"I blew her boyfriend to bits," I whispered. "He was all over her walls." My words didn't do justice to the horror I felt. Cold dread wrapped around my body, plummeting me into a shivering mass of flesh and bone.

Steve stepped into the bathroom doorway. "Damian said you might need me," he said, looking between the two of us before his gaze landed on my bloody hand. "What happened?"

"The demon attacked in a different way," I said, and his brow creased. It took a second and then his brow smoothed over.

"They went after Sandy?"

I nodded, pushing myself to my feet, and crossed to the sink, cleaning out the vile taste in my mouth before I started scrubbing the blood from my hand.

Steve hadn't said anything; he let me get myself in presentable order before he spoke.

"Tell me what happened."

"The bastard didn't possess her," I said to his concerned look and his shoulders relaxed.

"Thank god," he said and leaned on the doorframe waiting for the rest.

"He possessed her boyfriend," I said, and Steve straightened again, concern retracing the lines in his face. I looked at my healed palm. "He tried to bargain for my soul. When I said no, he slit her throat." I met his gaze and held up my clean palm. "Except I blocked it and then I stepped into the dorm room and blew him to bloody bits."

I held his gaze as he processed the information.

"And Sandy?"

"She's going to be a disaster for a while, but she's alive and now has one of Raven's necklaces to ward off evil spirits." I dropped my hand to the buttons on my ruined shirt, stripping it off and dumping it in the trash before heading to my room again. I stopped in the entry and stared at the droplets of my blood staining the carpet and turned toward my closet, pulling out another shirt. I wasn't sure what I was feeling right now.

Both Steve and Valerie left me at the entrance to my bedroom, heading downstairs and letting me have a little space to deal with what had happened. If I hadn't witnessed Raven's successful exorcism, I wouldn't be second guessing myself right now. Before that, a demon possession was certain death for the host, but knowing there was a way to save the guy, well, it just compounded the guilt and made me wonder if all my wrath was aimed solely at the demon. I probably could have vaporized him into dust, but I made a choice, however subconscious it was, to make a bloody fucking mess.

Chapter 21

"THIS HAS TO END. Now," I announced when I walked into the family room where everyone was sitting, enjoying each other's company. Silence blanketed the room, and all eyes locked on me. Valerie shook her head.

"You don't want to do what you're thinking," she said.

I ignored her, focusing on Damian. "How are the demons getting through from hell?"

He blinked at me and shrugged, and I moved my gaze to Steve's.

"If Paradise Cove is a portal to heaven, then Black Cove must be a gate to hell."

He paled, and so did Jennifer. "We closed that," he said, but the hesitation in his words belied the confidence in his statement.

"You killed one demon," I said. "But did you really close that gate?"

"I don't think it's one location," Damian said, thinking back on how easily Michael showed up wherever he was called. Lucifer could do the same before he was vanquished to hell.

"Demons aren't angels," I answered his train of thought. "They have to be escaping by some means, and from your memories, they existed back when you were turned. But they haven't overrun the earth, so they have to have limited access topside."

"They aren't escaping. They're following orders," Damian said.

"Either way, they're getting here through some sort of portal. It isn't through the same means that an angel has of just popping in whenever they damned well feel like it."

Faces stared at me with vacant eyes and the anger in my soul flushed a heat over my skin that scalded. I had to stop this madness. I would not live in fear for the rest of my life and the only way to do that, was to do what I had said to Valerie in the car.

I was going hunting.

I turned toward the closet and pulled out my coat. "They want a fucking war. They got one."

Steve shot to his feet and grabbed my arm before I got out the garage door.

"Don't," he started, and I yanked the fabric out of his grip.

"I have to. We..." I twirled my finger around, pointing to everyone in the house. "We will never know peace if I don't do this."

"Chris," Valerie said, approaching me.

I turned my angry gaze in her direction. "I want the fucking fairytale."

She stopped her approach and just stared, pleading with her beautiful eyes, and I gritted my teeth.

"It's hunting season," I growled, repeating the words my father had said many years ago. I glanced at the sudden paleness in Steve's cheeks before turning away. I didn't wait for a reaction; I stormed to my car and slid inside, willing everything in my way to yield. When the garage door opened, I had a clear path out of the house and I punched the gas, leaving a spray of gravel, dirt, and exhaust in my wake.

Each mile that passed ratcheted my anger and people on the highway gave me a wide berth, and in some ways, I felt like Moses parting the Red Sea. The power smashed through my veins in time with my heartbeat and throbbed in my temple. By the time I pulled into the driveway at the cottage, I was in an all-out frenzy.

I had never ventured to Black Cove and the only way I knew how was by following the small brook from Paradise cove. I trudged across the snow toward the lake and slowed at the singe spot, growling low in my throat at the sight of it. He was still messing with our lives, and I was damned if I'd allow that.

I stomped through the trodden path to Paradise cove where the moss was still clear and the ice at the edge of the water was thinning enough to see the water underneath. I turned my back on the beautiful prisms in the water and focused on the stream trench that disappeared to the right of the entrance.

"You will not win with that much anger ruling your emotions," the voice broke over the cove like soft rain, shocking every nerve in my body. I turned and swallowed the sudden lump in my throat.

"I have to try," I said, staring into my father's preternatural eyes and he smiled that knowing smile that bit under my skin.

"I know you do. But you've got to get a handle on your fury, otherwise, they'll use it against you. I really don't want to see you up here yet... if you get my drift. Neither does your mother. She wants grandkids," he said and flashed that smile again. "So do I."

Just seeing him reinforced my belief that the portals exist.

"Is Black Cove the only one?" I asked, and he shook his head.

"There aren't many, just a few dozen around the world," he added. "But trust me when I say they're harder to find than Black Cove is," he said with a sigh. "I know they exist, but I don't know where they are."

I nodded and turned away, stepping toward the woods.

"Son?"

I glanced back at him.

"I'm proud of you," he said.

"I haven't done anything, yet," I said, and he faded into the layer of fog that crawled across the ground. Leave it to my father to make me feel completely inadequate when I needed strength. I stepped off the moss into the snow, willing the thick brush to yield to my passage. I couldn't have cut a cleaner path had I had a machete in my hand, and I used the time to build the power and temper the fury to the point rational thought ruled.

As I got closer to Black Cove, the air thickened. Unwelcomed fear licked my skin, leaving it tacky under my coat, and I shifted. If my father could show up in Paradise Cove, could Lucifer appear in Black Cove? I glanced down at the chain holding the pendant over my heart and prayed that if Lucifer appeared, that chunk of rock would protect me from having my heart ripped out.

The combination of fear and fury does funny things to a man. With each step, my heart drove faster, and the evilness of the landscape penetrated my coat, chilling me and drawing sweat from my pores. I knew the distance was a little under a mile, but in the thick brush, it seemed longer, and I had a new appreciation for Steve.

He'd carried Jennifer's unconscious body the entire way, without the benefit of any supernatural powers, to cut a clear path. He ran on tenacious willpower alongside the drive to get her to safety, and he nearly bled out.

The forest echoed with unfamiliar noises, some sounding more like screams of the dead than forest creatures, and I slowed, knowing I was approaching the perimeter. The stench of brimstone settled on the air, and I put my hand to my nose to stop an unwanted sneeze. The last thing I wanted to do was announce my presence in the area.

I closed my eyes, pulling the details of the landscape from Steve's sketchy memories. If I mapped out my approach correctly, I would come in on the narrow path next to the sinkhole. There was no maneuverability if I was attacked there, and I had a feeling that sink hole wouldn't be a pleasant place to fall into.

I thought about just sending out a rolling wave of destructive power across the landscape, clearing it clean; but that was unreasonable, especially if I miscalculated and went farther than the reach of Black Cove. Killing a human being wasn't on my to-do list. I had done it once, granted it was warranted, but it still haunted me to this day.

Which left me the option of cutting through the thick woods until I was parallel with Black Cove's rotting moss bed. A twig snapped to my left, and I froze. Demons weren't the only things Lucifer commanded, and I set a deadly cocoon around me. If anything grabbed for me, they'd find themselves roasted to a crispy corpse.

I slogged my way through the woods, quietly carving the path. I'm sure my electrified safety net was enough of a disturbance to announce my presence, but I kept my thoughts masked. I curved back towards the cove, ignoring the drop in temperature. My adrenaline acted as a body warmer, setting my blood on overdrive enough so that even my palms were covered in a light sheen of sweat.

The dense forest thinned, and I saw my first slivers of the setting sun penetrating the trees. A thread of fear bit into me. I really didn't want to be here after dark and looking at the progression of the dying rays, I knew I wouldn't have a choice. Twilight was on the horizon and with it would come things just as nasty as demons.

Chapter 22

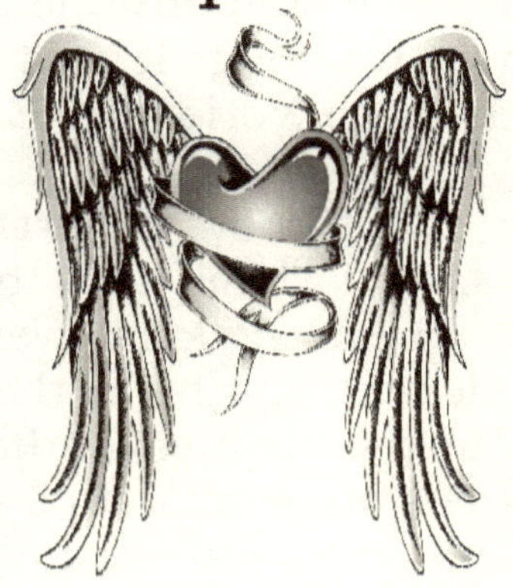

THE MOMENT I STEPPED onto the black moss, I knew I'd made a mistake coming alone. There must have been fifty demons just waiting for me and when I breached their domain, they parted, one by one, stepping to the side until I faced Lucifer's back.

Every memory of Damian's flooded my brain, terrifying me, and when he turned in my direction, I had to get a hold of the fear, otherwise I was going to pee my pants like a scared little kid. My gaze dropped to the gaping hole in his chest, and I shivered.

When the first demon reached out and actually touched my shirt, my heart leaped in my throat. My safety net was gone, and now I was at their mercy. Muscle memory guided my every move, parrying blows away, executing throws and kicks powerful enough to kill an ordinary man. I don't know how many I took down, but they just kept coming and my knuckles were scraped and bloodied by the blows I got in.

The muscles in my arms burned, but I kept going, snapping bone and dropping demons. But they didn't stay down long. It was like battling a horde of zombies from World War Z and I was one in a sea of many.

Most of them didn't know the art of self-defense, so I had that going for me, but that's where my benefits ended. These fuckers were strong and relentless. The demon spirits in their bodies were not susceptible to the frailties of the human body. Unfortunately, the same couldn't be said for me.

I faltered, and the first actual blow hit my kidney, driving me to my knees. I rolled into an empty space and dodged another blow, trying like hell to let loose some of the destructive power locked within my flesh. Nothing happened and the first tendrils of panic settled in, making my strikes less effective and my blocks either too early or too late. I couldn't seem to regain my center and each blow that connected had one goal; to break what it hit. I missed the next block, and a fist connected with my ribs, cracking at least two of them by the crushing pain.

I bellowed my pain, striking out and breaking a nose before stumbling back with my arm locked over my side to protect them from being hit again. I didn't get my arm up in time and a fist smashed my lips, splitting both of them and loosening several teeth, but I remained on my feet, shaking off the shock.

I knew if I went down, that would be the end; I wouldn't get back up.

The next blow smashed my cheek, and I stumbled, losing the battle with gravity. I landed on the side with the cracked ribs and yelled out. Pushing to my hands and knees, I tried to dodge the kick coming at me and served only to give someone on the other side a better shot of my back.

I curled and covered my head, screaming through the pain as over a dozen boot clad feet connected with my body. And then everything stopped. For a moment I thought I'd died. Then hands grabbed my arms, lifting me and bringing me back with a ferocious dose of agony.

Each step they took sent a jolt through my body and I couldn't help the tears. I'd welcome blacking out right now, but I knew if I did that, Lucifer would take control over my body, knocking my soul who knows where and the world would end.

They dropped me on the ground in front of Lucifer and I struggled to my hands and knees. One of his lackey bastards grabbed a fistful of my hair and pulled my head back.

"You're on my turf now, boy, or hadn't you noticed?" Lucifer asked, and I just stared at him. He crouched down in front of me. "You can end this. All you have to do is surrender," he said in a perfectly reasonable tone. He tilted his head and studied me like a poor lost stray.

"Fuck you," I hissed, spraying blood with my words.

"You sure about that? You think you're in pain now. I can make it infinitely worse." He stood, towering over me.

A cloud passed over the path of the dying sun, creating a dark shadow on the trees behind Lucifer that reminded me of an eagle... or a hawk, and I blinked the sudden vertigo away. I let out a raspy laugh at what must be a last-ditch hallucination. I was sure I was one punch away from death anyway, and if I died, my powers went with me.

"Game on, motherfucker," I glared through my only open eye, energized by the strength of my voice. It reminded me of my father and his steel nerves.

Lucifer gave a nod and the hands holding me disappeared. I dropped to my hands and knees and a painful flare from impact seized my muscles and I groaned. My forehead dropped to the ground, landing on the scratchy moss. Instead of clenching my eyes closed, I scanned the number of shoes surrounding me and forced an inhale. Too many for me to fight off, but I would not die kneeling on the ground. Lucifer's black steel toe boots circled me, and I pushed up, forcing myself to my feet, blocking the pain from overriding me. When he appeared in my peripheral vision, I turned my gaze toward him, stepping into form. I spit a wad of blood on the ground and glared in his direction.

If I couldn't influence matter around me, I damned well could look inward. The power was still there, brewing in my chest, filling my skin with the ability to remain standing. Tapping my mental reserve, I filled every inch of my broken body with strength and narrowed my good eye at him.

"Let's see what you got."

He tilted his head and my pinky snapped, pulling a groan from my chest that I clamped between my teeth.

I glanced at my pinky, willing the bone to reset, and damned if it didn't. It was still broken, but not at an angle. I couldn't curl into a fist. I did just that and smiled my best 'fuck you' smile.

"I may not be an archangel, but I'm a force to be reckoned with."

Lucifer leaned his head back and laughed and I threw a punch aimed at his throat. My fist stopped less than an inch away and my arm slowly twisted, peeling a growling scream from my throat when both my ulna and radius snapped. Flashes of light filled my vision, and I blinked them away even as he continued to twist.

"Your powers are useless here," he smiled as I kneeled helplessly at his feet, watching the skin tear around the breaks.

"His may be, but mine aren't," a familiar voice rocked the landscape, and the smell of singing moss filled my nostrils. The crowd surrounding us evaporated to dust, leaving Lucifer, Damian, and me on the playing field.

Lucifer let go of my arm and I collapsed to the ground, pulling the pieces to my chest. My breath wheezed in and out and I did the same thing I did with my finger, screaming my pain to the heavens. I clung to consciousness by a thread as the last direct rays of the sun disappeared.

Lucifer's boot pressed down on my throat and black spots filled my vision. My father's words echoed in my head and tears leaked from the corner of my eyes. He would be so disappointed in me for dying like this.

Something inside me broke, and with it whatever wall blocked my ability to harness and wield the power engulfing me shattered into a million pieces, and I let loose like I have never done, knocking Lucifer across the Cove. I struggled to my feet, unable to harness this fury or the fire ripping through my skin.

Damian's expression matched the absolute shock on Lucifer's face. The ground shook under us, crumbling under Lucifer's feet. Trees started toppling, sucking into the sinkhole, scraping the evil off the land and filling it with white light.

I had a moment, a quick glimpse through Damian's eyes, and what I saw fueled the power. I shined like a celestial being, one made to purify the land, and I was hell bent on destroying this portal, even if I lost my life doing it.

If I could destroy Lucifer in the process, that was just a bonus.

He charged at me, and I put my hand up like a traffic cop, targeting the power. I don't think he knew what hit him and he went down into the giant crack like a fly slapped in a hurricane. Trees amassed over the crevice, crackling and snapping as the white light surrounded us, peeling away the evil and scrubbing the land from edge to edge. Every bit of shrub and moss scraped down to the dirt, and the debris slid into the giant whirlpool where the sink hole had been, slipping through the crack until there was nothing left, and then the crack slammed closed, fused with light, closing this portal to hell forever.

The light faded, and I stared at the perfectly round, perfectly flat, and perfectly clean patch of land that reminded me of those strange alien crop circles in the mid-west. None of the devastation remained and what was left waited for a harvest of new life. I turned my gaze to Damian.

"So that's what happens when I lose control," I whispered, and then everything went black.

Chapter 23

MUFFLED SOUNDS AND DARKNESS.
Sobbing, then silence.
Bright light, then blackness, again.
A steady machine-like beep.
Hushed whispers.
Music.
Moments lost in the dark.
Where the hell was I?
Who the hell was I?
All fractional pieces of the puzzle that my brain couldn't wrap around.
There were no answers, just darkness and silence and nothing.

Chapter 24

I OPENED MY EYES, and everything around me was a blur. After a few blinks I stared at a hanging bag of liquid. The slow drip captivated me.

Drip, drip, drip.

I peeled my eyes away and turned my head. Lights bounced across a screen, just as hypnotizing as the drip above me. Spike up, back down, pause, spike again over and over like an endless steady earthquake. It took a few minutes for me to connect the timing of the spikes to the pounding in my chest. I moved my hands to the source and a hard smooth object lay in the spot I thought my heart should be and then my fingertips slid off whatever it was onto warm skin.

My brain was slow to understand, and it was a struggle to think clearly.

My nose tickled, and I reached up to scratch it, pulling small tubes from my nostrils. I stared at the thing, blinking as air flowed into my eyes. Why was it so hard to know the words for things? I turned my head away from the machines and they landed on a man slumped in a chair.

I didn't recognize him, just like I didn't recognize names for the things around me. Should I know him? Logic wasn't working, and I shifted uncomfortably in the bedding. His eyes blinked open, and he stretched, rubbing his scruffy face. Then his gaze landed on me, his eyes widened and met my gaze, and then widened some more.

"EA?" he said, and my brow creased. "O o ow whe oo a?" he asked, and his hands moved along with his speech, none of which made a lick of sense.

I blinked, hoping something would compute, but nothing came, and I just stared at him, unable to decipher what the hell he was saying.

He pulled something from his pocket and tapped the screen before turning it to me. It was covered with unfamiliar symbols strung together. Nothing registered.

Distant whispers filled my head, and I glanced around the room for the source and then back at the man. I shook my head slowly.

"Do you know where you are?" the question formed in my head an unfamiliar voice along with my own broken narrative. The man's mouth didn't move, and I glanced around the room, looking for the source.

He took my hand and my gaze snapped to him as I tried to pull my hand away.

He let go and pointed to his chest. *"CJ, it's me, Tom."*

I licked my lips and tried out the last word of the sentence. "Tom?" It came out in a harsh croak, and he smiled, nodding. It didn't hold any meaning, and I glanced around again for what made the words inside my ears.

Liquid sloshed, and I glanced back at him as he moved something clear with a thin plastic rod toward my mouth. I backed away, uneasy by the offering. The complete unfamiliarity of everything was pushing me closer to the freak out zone.

"*Take a small sip,*" the voice said as the plastic touched my lips.

I hesitated, unsure of what a sip was, and the man pulled the liquid away slowly, plugging one end of the plastic with his finger and placing the long straight end against my lips. He lifted his finger and cool liquid seeped into my mouth, quenching the dryness. I swallowed and closed my eyes, licking the remaining liquid from the corner of my lips.

"*Do you know where you are?*"

The voice announced again, and my eyes opened, scanning what I could see of the room before slowly shaking my head and dropping it back on the soft pillow.

"*You're at the hospital,*" the voice echoed softly in my mind, but his lips still didn't move. Again, I looked for the voice in my ear, but only the man stood in the room with me.

"Hos…pit..tal?" I tried the word out and it didn't come as smoothly as in my head. His smile faded.

"*Do you know who I am?*" the voice whispered and behind it resided pain that I couldn't identify. The man patted his chest when I didn't answer, his eyes pleading for a reaction that I couldn't give.

I stared at him and shook my head. The devastation in his eyes squeezed my heart, and he sat down slowly in the chair. That's when I realized he was the one talking in my head.

"*I'm your brother,*" his voice whispered.

"Broth…ther?" I asked, the meaning lost to me. I didn't know why it was so damned hard to speak or to understand things; it was like my brain wasn't firing on all cylinders.

He nodded. *"Do you know who you are?"* his voice invaded my mind again.

This time, I met his worried stare. "Bro...ther?" I said, because I had no idea what the right answer was.

He covered his mouth and his eyes glossed over with a watery sheen. When his eyes closed, some of the liquid leaked out, rolling down his cheeks. He opened his eyes and turned away with the device in his hand, tapping away at the screen for what seemed like ages. When he was done, he set his shoulders and turned, offering a smile meant to reassure, but it just scared the shit out of me.

Everything about this scared the shit out of me. Not being able to smoothly answer the questions or understand where I was scared the shit out of me, and my gaze darted around the room, looking for an escape route.

He reached over and picked up a stick that lay near my hand and pressed a red button on the top. I stared at the magic wand in his hand, trying to understand how I knew the button was red, or the fact that it was a button, for that matter.

The door opened and a woman with a white coat came in. She had her hair pulled back and her eyes, her eyes captivated and calmed me. The colors in her eyes swirled as she crossed the distance. The warmth in her gaze wrapped around me like a security blanket and I knew with her I was safe.

"Chris?" she asked in such a tender way that my heart ached for her. When she sat on the edge of the bed and took my hand in hers, I stared at the union of our flesh, and heat tingled from the point of contact through my form, from my head to my toes and everywhere in between. A living connection between the two of us created a warmth deep in my soul and even though I didn't remember her, I remembered this overwhelming and pure sensation.

"Hi," I croaked and blinked again. That word came from nowhere and the reaction seemed to sadden her.

Water sprang from her eyes, and then the right word popped into my head. She was crying, and those glistening drops were tears. I don't know why, but I sat up and pulled her into my arms. Holding her felt like home, and I closed my eyes, inhaling her sweet scent.

"Jesus, Chris, I didn't think you'd ever wake up," she whispered in my ear.

"Je..sus. Chri..is?"

She stiffened in my arms and slowly pulled away, the same concern present on her face as the man who called himself brother. She unwrapped from me and put her hand on my chest.

"Chris, that's your name," she said, blinking away the tears. She took my hand and placed it under the ornate necklace onto her flesh. "Valerie. I'm Valerie."

I stared at my hand on her chest. Underneath the soft warmth, her heart beat against my hand, echoing my own, and I knew this girl had a piece of my soul. It wasn't from a memory or familiarity; it was as natural as the air and just as essential to my survival.

And best of all, I knew the word to describe it.

"Val...er...ie." I glanced into her eyes. "Lo...ove Val...er...ie."

She got the meaning right away despite my stilted speech, and her eyes filled with tears. Her hand fluttered to her lips, and she nodded before leaning forward and placing a kiss on my forehead.

A strange tingle encompassed my head along with flashes of pain, of white light, of angels. The tingles cascaded down my body all the way to my toes and another word surfaced.

I tilted my head.

"Ha...avad?"

She let out a musical laugh and squeezed my hand. "Yes. I'm going to Harvard Medical School. I've already finished the classroom portion, with straight A's mind you, and now I'm in my second year of clinical rotations at the Children's Hospital."

She positively beamed, but something didn't compute right in my mind. Some important piece of information was missing, and I needed it to fix this awful dread in my stomach. I glanced at the man again and something clicked.

"Gr..grace?" I asked, and my brows rose. I wasn't sure the meaning, but it seemed important enough for me to voice.

"She's fine," Valerie said, and while my shoulders relaxed, it didn't stop the building trepidation. She glanced at the gadget on her wrist. "They should be here in an hour or so." She picked up my wrist and stared at the same band she did a minute ago and then sighed, meeting my gaze again. "You don't remember much, do you?"

I tilted my head and put my hand back on her chest. "Love. I re..mem...ber." My tongue wasn't articulating as quickly as I wanted, and Tom moved his hands again.

"I don't know," she said, meeting his gaze.

"Don...'t know?"

"If you'll ever regain your memory," she answered, and her eyes misted again.

I thought about her words and looked around the room, specifically at the pictures covering the opposite wall. "Ho...ow lo...ong?" I pointed to the bed.

She took my hands and met my gaze. "A little over two years."

I blinked, unsure of what that really meant. I'm sure what she said would mean something sooner or later, but right now it had all the sense of what an hour was.

"Mind fuck," I said, clear as day, pleased that something came out without the halting lilt, and she actually giggled.

"Big time," she said and leaned in, pressing her lips to mine. Everything stopped, no sound, no sensation other than her lips on mine and it felt right as rain. When the kiss broke, I smiled. The little machine clipped to her pocket beeped, and she glanced at the scrolling symbols.

"I have to go, but I should be back before everyone gets here, okay?" She palmed my cheek.

I took her hand and put it on my chest, forcing the question out. "Lo...ove Chri...is?"

She stared at her hand and then my eyes and I swallowed with the sudden understanding her answer to my question was where the dread originated. If she didn't, I might as well crawl back into the nothingness that came before this room.

She leaned close and kissed my cheek.

"Yes, Chris. I still love you. I always will." When she pulled away, I bit my lip and nodded, fearing the sting in my eyes.

She caressed my cheek and smiled. "I have to go now, okay?"

"O...kay."

The minute she left the room, an emptiness filled me like the other half of my soul was now gone and I looked at the man. "Valer...ie?"

"Ya," he said.

I searched for the words. "Come...back?"

He folded his hands in his lap and nodded. I got a whiff of a memory from him. He'd had to relearn how to communicate, too, and my gaze dropped to his hands, and I closed my eyes.

"Sign?" I said and popped my eyes open.

"Ya," he said and pointed to his mouth. "*No tongue. I had to learn sign language. It was a bitch not being able to talk,*" he thought. "*But at least you didn't have to wait for me to go through the pains of trying to spell shit out with my hands.*"

I nodded but didn't really understand, and then I put my hand to my chest. "Chri...is."

He nodded and put his hand on his chest. "*Tom.*"

The connection to the first time he referred to the name clicked, and I said, "Tom. Bro...other."

"Ya," he said aloud and took the seat. "*Do you understand what brother means?*"

Before I told him I didn't, the door opened and a man wearing the same type of thing Valerie wore walked in.

"Hi," I said, and he glanced at the chart in his hand.

"Welcome back, Mr. Ryan," he said.

I put my hand to my chest. "Chri...is," I forced the word out.

His gaze traveled from mine to Tom's and Tom's hands started speaking their language. The doctor nodded and took the pen out of his pocket, scribbling on the chart before focusing on me again.

"Your brother said you're having a problem remembering things and difficulty speaking. That's quite normal for people waking from extended comas." He approached and did the same thing with my wrist that Valerie did. "Since you seem to be awake now, I can remove some of the tubes attached and we can see if you can walk, okay?"

"Okay," I said and shrugged.

He checked a bag attached to the bed and then looked at me. "You're going to feel a little pressure," he said and then folded the sheets back. He pulled on a pair of gloves and handled me, gently pulling on the tube that seemed to grow out of me.

Pressure, holy fuck, it was more like a burning fire line. "Oww," I said and then was rewarded with relief when the plastic thing disappeared. He straightened the sheet back into place and snapped the gloves off.

"Not the most comfortable of things, I'm sure, but it was necessary. I'm going to leave the I.V. in until we see how you do with food." He pointed to the bag.

"O...kay," I said.

"Do you think you can get up?"

"U...p?" I asked, not sure of what he meant. The fact that I should know this stuff just added a low level of frustration.

The doctor sat on the edge of the bed and then straightened. "Up."

I nodded and swung my legs over the side of the bed. He put his hand out for support and I stared at it a second before pushing off the bed myself. My feet landed on the floor and the chill of the tile seeped through my socks. I straightened like he had.

His brows creased. "Take a step." He showed me what he meant.

I did as he asked.

"Another."

I took another step, and he flipped open the chart, scribbling again. With no more direction, I crossed toward the pictures on the wall, but I was stopped by something in my arm. I stared at the tube holding me to a minimal distance from the bed. It ran from my arm to the bag of liquid.

"Out?" I asked, pointing at the thing and meeting the doctor's gaze.

"Not yet," he said and went back to scribbling.

Irritation flushed through me, and I stared at it again. "Pft," I said and yanked the blue connector. The tube separated, and I dropped the end onto the bed, crossing to the wall and tracing the pictures with my fingers.

"Mr. Ryan, we need to put the IV back in," the doctor said, and I met his gaze, shaking my head. He stepped toward me, and Tom put his hand up, stopping the doctor. Whatever his hands conveyed, the doctor gave a curt nod and left us alone.

Tom stepped next to me. *"Damian's kids drew those for you."* he thought, and I met his smiling gaze with no reference point to understand his commentary. *"Grace did this one."* he pointed to a vibrant angel drawing.

"Gr...ace?" I ran my hand along the waxy surface.

He nodded and his smile faded. *"I've got a little girl now, too,"* he thought. *"Her name is Hannah."*

"Han..n...ah?"

His eyes swam in a sheen of tears. *"I wish you had been awake when she was born."*

Tom turned away, and I grabbed his arm, struggling for the right word to say, and then the light bulb went off. "Con...gra." I closed my eyes, frustrated that I was having so much difficulty. I focused on the word, concentrating. "Con...grat...tu...la..tions." I smiled and opened my eyes.

He pressed the tips of his fingers to his lips and brought them down into the palm of his other hand. *Thank you* resounded in my head. A layer of comfort settled over me as I stared at him. I still remembered nothing, but I felt the kinship in his heart.

"I'm so...rry I..." I couldn't think of the right string of words that came after that and I looked at the ceiling for a little help. "There?" I glanced at him and bit the side of my lip.

He didn't speak, instead he pulled me into a hug. I awkwardly patted his back and when he pulled away, he crossed to the window and wiped his face. Glancing one more time at the wall, I sighed and headed back to the bed, climbing in and looked at the dripping tube.

"Help?"

Tom turned, and I held up the tube. He reached and pushed the red button again.

A few minutes later, a nurse came in and her eyebrows arched at me sitting up in the bed. "You're awake," she said, and I nodded without rolling my eyes at the obvious. I held up the IV lead in one hand and showed her the base plug in my hand, raising an eyebrow, hoping she'd know what the hell I was trying to convey. My thoughts seemed to come together more, but the trigger to my mouth was still shoddy at best.

She seemed to recover and crossed, her gaze moving to Tom's back at the window.

"Well, since you seem to be moving, maybe we can get you cleaned up? Would you like that?"

"Cl...ean?"

She paused, and Tom turned. I met his gaze, and he gave me a slight nod. *She's asking if you want to take a shower. It's probably not a bad idea.*

"Okay," I said. I seemed to have mastered that word and my assent pleased her.

"We can leave that out until we're done," she said.

"We?" I blinked as she helped me to my feet.

"Well, I can't leave you in there by yourself," she said in a perfectly reasonable tone.

I glanced at Tom for help, but he just smirked and turned back toward the window.

"I...my...self," I said with a little more force and stepped away from her.

She studied me standing on my own and then met my gaze. "I'll let you wash yourself, but I need to be in there with you."

"N...no."

"I," Tom said, pointing to his chest and crossing the distance. He spoke with his hands.

"If something happens," she argued, and his hands flew through another explanation I didn't understand.

She looked at me. "Your brother will stay with you in the bathroom, and I will wait just outside the door. Does that work for you?"

I nodded and trudged into the room she pointed to and stared at the open stall and the dials on the wall beyond the entrance. The logistics of taking a shower seemed foreign, and I glanced over my shoulder at Tom.

He sighed and closed his eyes, sending me a picture of what he did in a shower. It seemed reasonable, and I peeled the hospital gown off and pulled the paper undergarments off as well as my socks, leaving it on the floor and stepped inside the shower stall, waiting.

Tom reached beyond me and touched the control. *Pull and turn this way for hotter water,* he thought and hooked his thumb toward the entrance, *and that way for cooler water.* He pointed toward the back of the shower. He picked up a bottle. *Shampoo for your hair.* And after putting that down, he pointed at the small square bar. *Soap for your body. Got it?*

"Thi...ink so." I said and waited until he stepped away and then pulled the knob, turning it toward the entrance. Warm rain fell from the spout, but it got hot enough to scald, and I realized I was turning the knob the wrong way and quickly dialed it the other way. I was rewarded with frigid water. Shivering, I slowly turned the dial back until the water hit the perfect temperature.

I stepped under the stream, closing my eyes and letting the water pound my face and chest. Sensations returned along with a glimpse of another shower at another time. My eyes shot open, and I tried to force the memory. The penalty for trying to pull blood from a stone was the slam of vertigo. I reached for the wall and Tom's hand grabbed my wrist, giving me a steadying hold.

I sent a weak smile in his direction and repeated the hand gesture he used to say thank you. He gave me a nod and released his grip with his eyebrows rising in a question. I nodded. I would be okay as long as I didn't pry my mind open with brute force.

Another inconvenient truth occurred after the shampoo suds flowed into my open eyes. It was a stinging lesson to always close your eyes when you're rinsing shampoo from your hair. The grin that formed on Tom's lips prompted me to raise my middle finger at him. It was an automatic reaction, and I stared at my finger as he broke out into a snorting laugh. I turned and rinsed my stinging eyes out before making sure no stray soap was still in my hair. When it squeaked between my fingers, I gathered it was clean.

Once I seemed to have cleaning my hair mastered, I took the bar of soap in my hands and ran it over my chest. The clean scent filled the steam-filled enclosure, and I followed the silent instruction Tom had given me. When I was done and the soap returned to the dish, I just stood under the spray, letting it pelt my back.

I sent a smile to Tom, and he returned it before twirling his finger. I knew the gesture, but I wasn't sure what it meant. I tilted my head and scrunched my brow.

Wrap it up.

I pushed the knob, and the water shut off. Tom handed me a towel, and I dried off with little instruction. I even wrapped the towel around my waist without help. We stepped back into the room.

"Cl...ean." I said to the nurse.

"Did you brush your teeth?" She pointed to her teeth, and I shook my head. She grabbed me by the elbow and led me back into the bathroom. A tube and a little brush sat on the counter, and she picked it up, lining it with a dab from the tube and handed it to me. I pulled it to my mouth and followed the motions she was doing with her finger on her own teeth.

The minty taste filled my mouth, creating a pleasant tingle.

"Now spit in the sink and rinse the brush."

I spit and tentatively reached for the controls on the faucet. When I successfully turned it on and did what she said, I replaced the brush where she picked it up.

She grabbed a towel and wiped my lips before swiping it across the steamy wall, revealing her reflection along with Tom near the door and another man. It took me a moment to realize the blue eyes glued to the reflection were mine.

The nurse handed me another utensil, and I studied the thin tool.

"It's a comb. For your hair." She took it from my hand and ran it gently over the top of her hair from brow to crown and I nodded, taking it from her and doing the same until my hair was knot-free and slicked back. It wasn't much longer than Tom's and easy to manage.

"That's good. Let's see if we can find you something clean to wear, okay?"

I nodded and followed her into the room where Tom had already laid out a pair of underwear on the bed, along with thin pants and a shirt. Studying the different articles of clothing, I figured out the correct way to put the underwear on, along with the pants. I left the pull tie loose because after a couple of attempts; I didn't get how it clasped together.

The shirt slid on over my shoulders with buttons on the front, but I left it open.

The nurse stepped forward, reaching to help, and I stopped her.

"Not...co...old."

"All right," she said and led me back to the bed, helping me under crisp sheets.

I pointed to the bed. "Cl...ean?"

"Yes, I changed it while you were in the shower." She picked up the IV line and reattached it. "There you go," she said and patted my hand. "If you need to use the bathroom, this can roll with you now." She showed me I was no longer tied to the bed.

"Th...ank.....you," I said, along with the proper hand gesture.

She left with a smile, and I turned to Tom.

"Th...th.....is st..stut.....r.....g sucks."

He laughed and nodded. "Ya wo a mi." *Yeah, worse than mine.*

I raised my eyebrows. "De...b.....te." I inhaled, forcing the rest out. "Able."

He sat down and folded his hand over his fist, leaning it on his grinning lips.

Before I formulated another response, the door slammed open in a flurry of activity. The noise and chaos shocked fear into my blood and I pulled my knees closer to my chest in response, wrapping my hands around them and staring as a group of people poured in.

"Uncle CJ!" a little voice pierced the room and a small child broke free of her mother's hand, her coat flying off and landing a few feet away as she jumped, grabbed onto the rail, and climbed onto the bed.

Paying no mind to my raised knees, she squeezed between my chest and legs and plunked down in my lap, clapping her hands with joyful glee.

I didn't know whether to be horrified or humored by this, and I stared into the hauntingly dark eyes and smiled as her little hands cupped my cheeks.

"Grace, get off him," the woman from whom she broke free said.

"Gr...race," I said, and she nodded emphatically. "I like.. pic..tu...re," I added, pointing towards the wall.

She patted my cheeks and turned. "Mommy. Uncle CJ!"

I pulled my gaze away from the happy child on my lap and glanced at the group still piling in the door. Tom had joined a pretty red head holding a little swing from her arm. It took a second, but the word car seat came to my mind. Behind the red head stood a man who looked a great deal like Tom and confusion clouded my mind.

The sudden chaos overwhelmed me, and I didn't know where to look. I recognized no one and my heart started the fast pump of an unfathomable fear. Even the little girl bouncing on my lap presented mental challenges that made the room spin.

Grace placed her hands on my cheeks again, pulling my attention to her. There was no more smile gracing her lips, just a sad expression that further clouded my judgment and breathing got harder. Everything twisted into prisms, and I blinked. My vision righted, but small lines of heat rolled down my cheeks.

"It's okay," the child whispered.

"Guys!" the familiar voice cut through the noise.

My gaze snapped to Valerie standing in the doorway, a tray balanced on one hand and her other propped on her hip with an expression I wouldn't want aimed at me. Her gaze met mine and locked on there for a minute. The way they traveled down my chest and back up gave me that warm tingly feeling and I sent her the hand signal for thank you.

"Guys, you're overwhelming him," she said, stepping inside and closing the door behind her. She crossed and messed up Grace's hair before setting the tray on the little table to my right. "I brought you something to eat," she said before taking my hand and turning to the group. "Chris is awake, but he's suffering from regressive amnesia. He doesn't remember a thing before waking up here."

I opened my mouth to argue, and she shot me a 'shut up until I'm done' glare. I closed my mouth, meeting Grace's gaze. The smile was back, but it was tempered by my unease.

"That is also affecting his ability to speak," she added, and I nodded.

"Wo...ords h...ha...hard," I added, scanning the six adults standing at the foot of my bed. I glanced at Tom and the woman with the red hair. He had his arm around. His attention wasn't on me, it was on the baby in her arms.

"Han...nah?"

Tom looked up and smiled, taking the baby from the redhead and bringing her to me. *My daughter,* he thought, and Grace moved to my side while Tom placed the baby in my arms. It was so small and wiggly. I shifted and found a comfortable hold and she settled down, making a little squeal before Tom put a small pacifier in her mouth.

"Beau...bu." I closed my eyes. I knew what I wanted to say, but it was too complex for my mouth to form.

"Beautiful," Valerie whispered, and I opened my eyes, nodding, meeting her gaze. "Chris, this is our family." she gestured toward the now silent crowd.

"F...fam...il..ly?"

"Yeah, babe. Family."

"Oh," I replied and tried to remember. Even one memory would be a blessing, but it was a big black hole. I shifted the baby to my hands, handing her back to Tom.

"Don't force it, hon. It'll come."

What if it didn't? What if I never remembered my past with these people?

I closed my eyes for a minute and the sensation of falling hit. I jerked on the bed, grabbing the edges. My eyes popped open, and the panic came alive in my veins.

Valerie turned to the group. "I think maybe we should do this another day."

I didn't argue, dropping my gaze to my hands, fidgeting with the edge of the blanket as Valerie ushered them out, exchanging hushed whispers about my condition. She stepped back in and crossed the distance, taking a seat and pulling the tray closer.

"So...ory," I whispered, feeling as small as Grace.

She reached under my chin, tilting my head so I'd meet her gaze. "Never apologize for being overwhelmed."

"Wha.." I stopped and clenched my fists. "What if I nev..ver..."

She put the tips of her fingers on my lips, stopping me. "It takes time."

The mention of time got me thinking. "H..how...m...man...y hours," I paused a moment and took a breath to force the rest of my question out. "i...is tw...two ye...years?"

She sighed and her lips moved as she silently calculated it for me. "17,520 hours. You've been in a coma for a little over twenty thousand hours."

My brain couldn't wrap around that now that I knew what an hour felt like. I covered my face, running my fingers into my hair, trying to grasp it. Valerie stood and headed toward the door. I didn't want her to leave, and I glanced at the open door. It slammed closed. Something had leaped from my chest and the door closed.

I stared with my mouth open, and Valerie turned, propping her hands on her waist and gave me a look that reduced me to shame.

"I wasn't leaving. I was going to close the door."

"Oh," I studied my hands.

When she returned to my bedside, she pushed the tray aside and shooed me over on the mattress, taking a seat so she faced me. "The fact you survived was a miracle," she started and stopped, her eyes dropped to the spot right in front of her.

It was my turn to lift her chin.

"Even my ability to heal took time to put you back together," she said when our eyes met.

"Why d...on't I re...mem...ber you here?" I asked
and tapped my head. "Wh..hen I re...mem...ber you
here." I pointed to my heart. I didn't really expect
an answer, so when she spoke, I moved, pulling her
to me and crushing her lips against mine.

This time, her lips parted, and I followed her
lead. Our tongues entwined in the most sensual
kiss. Slow and lazy and breathless. She pulled away
when my hand dropped to her breast, caressing her
through the thin fabric.

"Someone could walk in," she said.

I looked at the door and then the ceiling as I
searched for the word I was looking for. "Lo...ock."
The word hiccupped from my lips but was perfectly
enunciated in my head and the click of the lock on
the door engaging made me smile and I turned back
to Valerie.

A smile gained traction on her lips.

I reached out and pulled the elastic out of her
hair before running both of my hands through her
dark satin locks. The silky feel of it caressed my
hands. I traced her face, memorizing the lines,
burning every sensation into my brain, so if I ever
lost my way again, I would know her anywhere.
When my thumb ran over her lips, she kissed it and
met my gaze.

"Are you going to kiss me or what?" she
whispered, her swirling eyes sparkled.

I licked my lips and curled my hand around the
back of her neck, guiding her toward me.
Sensations billowed over my skin, covering me with
a need that drove my actions. The kiss I delivered
started tentatively, stirring the molten lava in the
center of my being. I moved from her lips to under
her jaw, finding a spot that made her shiver.

Running my hands under the lab coat, I peeled
it off, revealing a sleeveless V-neck shirt. I pulled

her into my lap and turned, laying her against the pillow before continuing my exploration of her. Each layer I peeled off of her brought more delights, and she never interrupted my studies. My fingers memorized her curves, and my tongue memorized her taste. Her spring-like musk tickled my nose and her soft purr recorded into my mind forever. She filled every one of my senses with awe.

Time meant nothing to me right now. All I wanted was this goddess.

I crawled back from my inspection of her finely painted toes with a hunger I couldn't categorize. She smiled at me and guided my hand between her legs. I circled the wet folds with my fingers, watching her mouth part and head tilt back when they ran over a certain spot. The effect her pleasure had on me was irresistible.

She widened her legs, and I smiled, leaning over and covering the area she liked best with my mouth, circling my tongue over the flesh.

"Oh, God, Chris," she said in a throaty sigh that coaxed me to continue the motion.

Her hand threaded into my hair, guiding me to the spot that quickened her breath. I slid my index finger inside her wet folds, slowly because I wasn't sure exactly what I was doing, but it all felt surreal and my senses were highly attuned to her.

"Faster," she whispered, and it took me a moment for the word to compute, but instead of honoring her request, I wasn't ready to set aside the physical study of what drove her crazy. I smiled and purposely slowed down. Sucking her in a way that pulled a moan from her chest.

"That's not faster," she said, her eyes half-crazy with delight.

"I know," I said, still rolling my tongue around her. The fact the words didn't stutter wasn't lost on either of us. My gaze dropped from her stormy eyes to her hard nipples, and I left my post between her legs, kissing my way up her body, much to her chagrin.

I kept my hand between her legs, circling the spots my tongue had while I covered each nipple with my mouth, sucking gently, and she arched into me, pulling me closer to her bosom.

When I found her lips, she kissed me with a fervor that sucked the air out of my lungs and left me as breathless as she was.

"Make love to me," she whispered when our lips parted.

"I am."

She peeled my shirt off, nipping at my neck as her fingers fumbled with my pants and couldn't quite reach to do anything more than shift the waistline. "Take your pants off," she said.

I leaned back on my knees and pushed them down as she instructed and stared at my hard member. I glanced up at her, unsure whether or not to be alarmed. Valerie smiled and reached for me, her hand gentle and soft around my skin as she stroked.

I entered the next stage of heaven when she guided me inside her. I stretched out, and she wrapped her legs around me, our hips moved in slow exquisite circles, my body entered sensory overload and I took her breast in my mouth, speeding up the sensations until I thought my heart was going to pound right out of my chest.

A wave started in my toes and rocketed up my legs, seizing every muscle and I groaned, burying my head into the crook of her neck. Spasms clenched me, making my body tremble all at once and then my muscles acted like I had been hit with a tranquilizer dart, slowly relaxing until all that was left was a trembling mass of flesh.

I lifted my head and met her gaze, and she pulled me to her lips. I moved the necklace and pressed my ear to her chest. The drum of her heart made my eyelids droop.

"Chris?"

"Mmm," I looked up at her.

"I need to get up," she said and pointed to the bathroom.

I rolled off her and watched as she slid off the bed, gathering her clothing. She headed into the bathroom without looking at me, and my euphoria faded. I pulled up my pants and tightened the strings, but again I couldn't figure out what to do with them.

The toilet flushed, but she didn't come out right away and I wondered if I had done something wrong. Instead of waiting, I slid off the bed and grabbed the rolling IV bar. I rounded the corner, and she stood leaning on the sink with her head down. Her shoulders shook.

"Val?" the shortened version rolled off my tongue easily, and she stiffened. Her head rose enough for me to catch a glimpse of her tear-stained face. "Di...id I do so...some...thi...ing wro...ng?"

She turned and shook her head. "You did everything right," she said.

I closed the distance. "Th...then wha...at?" I wiped the tears with my thumbs, searching her eyes for answers.

She let out a laugh. "You unhinge me,"

"So...or...ry"

"Please don't apologize for being perfect," she said.

It was my turn to laugh. Perfect? I knew what that meant, and she had to be the one with brain damage. I wasn't perfect by any means. I couldn't remember my family or even my full name and I couldn't speak worth a damn.

"Christopher James Ryan."

"Huh?"

"Your full name. Your family calls you CJ for short. I like your real name as opposed to the nickname. It's softer, sweeter." Her cheeks turned red, and she sniffled and turned back to the sink, splashing water on her face and then patting it dry with the towel.

"I think you'll be able to go home in a few days if you continue to do this well."

When she turned towards me, I stepped closer, looking down into her eyes, and pressed my palm to the warm flesh over her heart. "I am home."

Chapter 25

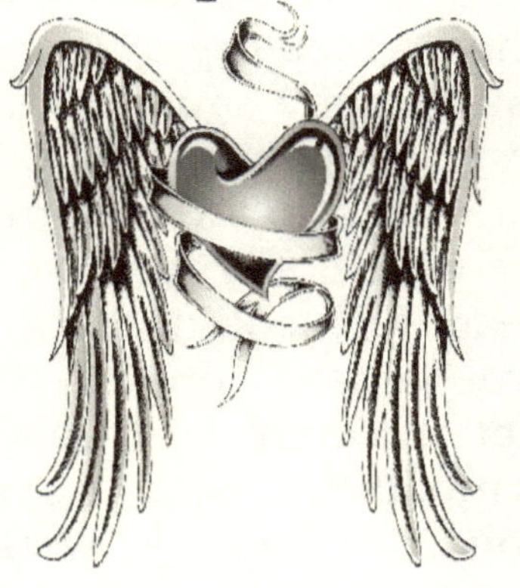

I WOKE TO A darkened room, disoriented. It took me a second to place where I was, and another to realize I was alone. Valerie was no longer in my arms like she had been when we fell asleep. I turned to the chair, expecting to see her curled on the cushion, but it was empty, and my heart skipped and pounded in my throat.

Pressure pushed down on my chest, and I glanced at the door. The lock wasn't engaged, and I slid out of bed, unsure of which direction to go. My body made the choice for me when the sudden urge to piss overshadowed my desire to find Valerie. I headed toward the bathroom and relieved myself, like Valerie had instructed last night. Before starting my search, I brushed my teeth and ran the comb through my unruly hair, putting it in some semblance of order. My gaze dropped to the medallion, and I ran my fingers over the black and red star before meeting my gaze. I studied my reflection, not finding any noticeable scar on my face or chest that would warrant dropping into the black for two years. With a shake of my head, I turned, collecting my pants off the floor and put them on before I ventured beyond the only environment I had a memory of.

Hesitation stalled my muscles as I opened the door to a brightly lit hallway. Quiet permeated the floor, but I could hear soft voices in the distance. I just wasn't sure which way they were coming from. I ducked my head out, looking both ways for a sign of where she would have gone. Given the choice of two non-distinct directions, I turned to my right, studying the symbols on the doors and the brightly colored lines on the floor. Artwork speckled the walls, most drawings by young hands, and I smiled as I passed a collection that reminded me of Grace's art.

The voice grew as I got closer to where the hall opened up to a bright area. A collection of nurses stood behind a desk on the left side of the atrium watching as a candy striper read to a group of children. I leaned on the entryway, listening to the story as the girl read. Halfway through the next page, she glanced up and her voice faltered as her gaze fell on me.

Some children looked over their shoulder at me, their heads in varying states of hair loss or covered with hats. Those that saw me turned back when the girl continued the story. To the right of the entrance was a large object that I couldn't find the right word for and in front of it sat a small bench. I crossed and took a seat, still able to see the girl, but my gaze dropped to the black and white ivory keys in front of me.

One child in the back got up and crossed to where I sat. She leaned on the edge or the instrument and asked, "Do you play?"

"I d...don...t know." My speech was still a crap shoot, and I offered a halfhearted shrug. "Wha...at is i...it?"

"It's a piano," she said and, shooed me aside.

I moved, giving her space on the bench and watched her place her thin fingers on the keys. "This is middle C." She pressed the note. I grinned at the melody of that one note and then she enthralled me more by playing a progression up and down the scale for me.

"My mom used to make me practice all the time." She ran through the scales and then pulled her fingers away and stared at me. "What's wrong with you?"

I shrugged and tapped my head. "No mem...m...or...y." Instead of trying to articulate the same question, I pointed at her and raised my eyebrows.

"Cancer," she said. "They think the chemo will help this time."

"I ho...pe so."

"Thank you. I gotta get back." She slid off the bench just as the girl closed the book.

My gaze dropped to the piano keys, and I placed my fingers on them, closing my eyes. My fingers moved of their own accord, filling the atrium with the slow cadence of music. I played the tune and then repeated it. Words flowed in time with the melody, softly at first and then drifting over the children. When I got to the chorus, more voices than my own joined me, singing Hallelujah, and I opened my eyes.

I didn't know where the words or the music were coming from, but I had no stutter and the rapt attention of everyone in the vicinity made me smile. I slid my gaze to the entryway that I had come from, and Valerie stood in the center with cups in her hands and her mouth open in surprise.

The children and some adults came closer. I continued, even as a rash of gooseflesh crawled up my arms and before long, everyone was singing with me. The rush of it created a heat in my cheeks and when I finished, silence blanketed the room for a minute before the clapping started.

I stared at my hands and then the people prompting me to play something else. Even the little girl who had told me this was a piano was egging me on. I glanced at Valerie and her paralysis broke. She crossed the distance.

"Okay, kids, Chris needs to go back to his room now," she said, and eyes turned to her.

"But Dr. Denongalis," one child whined, and she raised an eyebrow. The group collectively whined "aww" and disbursed.

"I didn't know you played," she said, staring at me before she handed me the cup.

I shrugged. "I di...dn't know, eith...ther."

Her eyebrow cocked. "That's my favorite song."

"Oh."

"And you sang it flawlessly." She took my elbow, leading me back toward my room. "Come on. You need to have some tests today to make sure everything is okay."

"Okay." I followed her back to the room, studying the walls again as I passed. "Why here?" I asked, pleased when the simple words came out without a stutter.

She glanced over her shoulder. "I wanted you where my rotation was. So, you're at Dana Farber in the children's section."

I thought about our escapades last night and heat filled my face. If I had known we were in the children's ward... ah hell, I still would have indulged. When we stepped into the room, the man who looked similar to Tom turned from his station at the window. My smile faded.

"You never told me Chris could play the piano," she said to him.

He let out a small laugh. "He doesn't."

With that, I was now the focal point of both sets of eyes.

"How did you do that?" she asked in just a small whisper.

I raised a shoulder. "I heard it in my head."

With a couple of blinks, she turned toward the man. "Chris, this is Steve. He's your father."

"I adopted you after your parents died," he added, clarifying his role further. "You and Tom have called me Uncle Steve ever since."

I gave him a nod, and my gaze dropped to the floor. "I don't remember you," I said, but the words didn't flow as smooth from my mouth as they did in my head. At least now the single syllable words didn't pause and restart like a stuck recording like the rest. I hated the fact that I was still struggling.

"It's okay," he said, his voice soft and low, and I looked up into his blue irises. "Valerie asked me to come because, if the tests show nothing to be alarmed about, she said, I can take you home."

I stepped back and my gaze slid to Valerie.

"If everything checks out, you can't stay," she said, the conflict in her eyes hammered against my chest.

"But?"

"I will see you at home when this rotation ends." Her stern eyes met mine in the same way she scolded the children a few minutes ago, but I knew under the sternness was hesitation.

It should have made me feel better that she didn't want me to go, but it didn't. As a matter of fact, I didn't like this at all. This was familiar and calm and the only normal I knew. Being with her was home. "How long?"

"I have another six weeks here."

"How man...ny hours?" I said because six weeks didn't mean squat to me.

"There are twenty-four hours in a day and seven days in a week." She crossed her arms.

The calculation in my head took the same time as it took her to cross her arms. "A thousand hours?" I gawked.

"One thousand and eight, to be exact," she said. "You can visit on weekends if you want," she said, and I nodded while the center of my body slowly twisted into a knot. "And we'll have to get you a piano."

The heat rose in my cheeks. I still didn't understand how I did that, but the way she looked watching me was worth going out and buying a hundred pianos. "When you come home," I said.

She sent a smile my way and handed me the shirt that hung over the end of the bed. "Time for us to take a look at your magnificent brain," she said, and I didn't meet Steve's gaze, but he did chuckle and took a seat in the chair, opening a tablet and settled in.

The machine was loud, and I had to stay still while it rattled around me. Valerie's voice kept telling me I was doing well, appeasing my unease with soft assurances every time the anxiety ratcheted up. The whispers of thought tickled my mind and while I didn't understand the terminology being used, I got the awe and excitement at what they saw.

I stared at the white plastic and the more I thought about leaving, the more the knot in my stomach clenched. The machine finally silenced, and Valerie came in, pulling me out of the scanner. Her gaze told me I was more than fine, and I closed my eyes. Sighing.

As we walked back to the room, I asked. "Before. How long did we…"

She slowed to a stop and met my gaze. "How long were we together before you got hurt?"

"Yes."

She sighed. "Three days."

"Three days?" The declaration sent a wave of chills through me. "What the fuck?"

She pulled me into an empty room. "Neither of us expected it at all. And in case you hadn't noticed, neither of us is what you would call normal. Normal people can't heal with a kiss or read minds or lock doors with a thought."

I crossed my arms and stared down at her, unconvinced. Even without much of a memory, I knew three days didn't make this kind of connection. It had to have been more.

"We shared memories," she finally said. "When we first touched, we got a download of each other's lives. It was a real mind fuck because, in a matter of seconds, it was like we were lifetime friends with a hell of a physical connection."

"How…" I didn't know how to articulate the question and stepped back, clenching my fists in frustration. "Three days?" I asked instead.

She nodded. "You were my first," she said, and I looked at her, blinking, trying to catch up. "Last night was my second time, ever." Her voice softened. "You aren't imagining the connection. I was lost for the last two years, walking around like half my soul was gone."

"But three days to be this…" I paused and swallowed, targeting the right word. "De…pen…dant?"

"It's not logical. But then again, you playing a song that I played at least a dozen times a week when you were in a coma, like you performed it a thousand times, isn't logical. You nearly dying..." she pressed her lips together and her mind closed with a slam.

"What happened to me?"

"You saved our lives," she said and stepped around me to the door.

I grabbed her arm, and she met my gaze.

"Seeing you so broken..." Tears filled her eyes, and she shook her head, unable to speak for a minute as her locked down memories overtook the conversation. She took a deep breath and continued, "I'm in love with you, Chris. I have been since you first kissed me. For me, it wasn't the memory download, it was that kiss. Time stopped and nothing existed but you and as much as I didn't want to, you stole my heart by believing in me like no one else ever had. I waited for you, not knowing if you'd ever wake up."

Tears painted her face. "You became home to me."

"You're my home." I leaned in and kissed her gently and accepted our bizarre attachment. I really had no choice. The thought of navigating life without her left me terrified.

Chapter 26

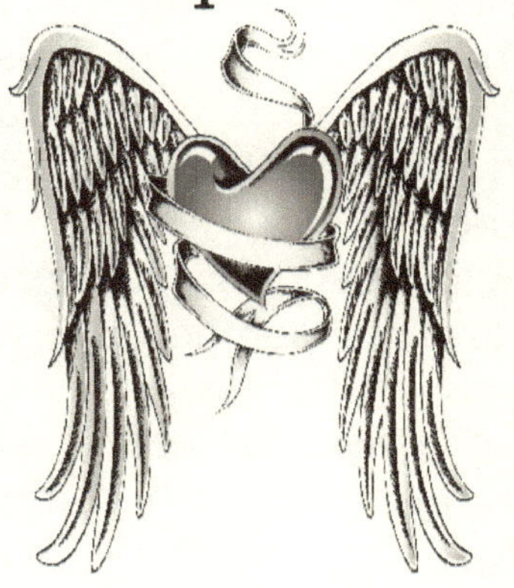

STEVE NAVIGATED THE CAR out of the parking lot and wound his way around the city until we pulled onto a wider road. Signs with symbols hung on the overpasses and we eventually turned off the two-lane highway in favor of a wider stretch. I still couldn't read, and I wondered just how long it would be until that ironed itself out. Instead of trying to study the roadways and signs that were as foreign to me as anything else, I studied the scenery for a while.

"Piano?" he said after a while.

"Yeah," I said.

"Huh," he huffed, shaking his head like that was the damnedest thing.

"What happened?" I asked, pushing the stilted words out.

Steve sighed and continued staring out at the road. "A lot," he finally said and glanced at me before focusing on driving.

I waited for more, but it was obvious nothing was coming. All I heard was a low-level static from him. "Are you really my uncle?"

He smiled and shook his head. "No. I met your father while I was on a case and we kind of grew on each other. Unfortunately, he was killed in the crossfire and your mother died later that same year. Murdered by the same wacko who nearly killed your brother."

"What do you do?" I stuttered, now more nervous to be around someone associated with so much death.

"I used to be a special agent with the Federal Bureau of Investigation. A cop," he added when I raised an eyebrow.

"Cop?"

He bit his lip, and the space between his eyebrows creased. "A cop keeps the peace and goes after the bad guys. Their job is to keep people safe," he said, trying to boil it down into simplistic terms.

"Valerie said I saved everyone's life. Does that make me a cop?"

"No. You aren't a cop." He glanced at me. "You're just a kid who stepped into something far worse than you could handle alone, and we nearly lost you."

"Why is everyone being so cryptic?"

He laughed. "It's our turn to keep you safe," he said and met my gaze. "Valerie doesn't think you're ready yet, and I have to trust the doctor's instincts."

I crossed my arms and sank farther into the seat, opting to watch the other cars on the road instead of engaging in any further conversation.

"Give it time," he said, pulling my gaze back to him. "It's been a rough road for all of us and we'd just like the chance for you to get to know us before we walk you through what happened. Okay?"

I caught the sheen of tears in his eyes, and he blinked them away without shedding any.

"Okay," I agreed.

He glanced at me. "You're doing a little better talking than you were yesterday," he said.

"Yes." I continued watching the scenery. "Small words work, the rest, not so much."

"Val said you still had an issue reading. Do you recognize any letters on the road signs?"

I glanced at the green signs with white symbols and shook my head. "No."

"Well, we'll have to work on that."

His matter-of-fact statement made me shift in the seat. "I don't understand how the words are in my head, but I can't remember what they look like."

"The brain is a funny thing." He glanced at me. "I assume you can still do some things you did before?"

I stared at him, hesitating for a moment before nodding. If Valerie trusted him enough to let him take me out of the hospital, then perhaps I should put some trust in the man.

He gave me a soft smile. "I used to have some of that magic mojo," he said and sighed. "The illusion of invincibility was a comfort most of the time and reading Jen's mind was always an adventure." He laughed. "It's been an adjustment not having it anymore."

"What happened?"

Steve sighed. "Valerie. She was sick and in order for Damian and me to get her out of danger, I had to heal her." He was quiet for a bit. "It was kind of the same thing that happened to me when I first..." he trailed off, searching for the right word. "Absorbed your older brother's powers. It was as much of a shock to him as it had been for me."

"Tom?" I asked, focusing in on the word brother.

"No, Eric. He died the same year as your parents."

"You sure seem to be around a lot of dead people," I said.

He laughed. "True, and some stick with you longer than others." His laughter wound down and there was an emptiness about him that etched into the lines of his face. "Silence is another thing I've had to get used to."

"Huh?"

"The constant undercurrent of thoughts of those around you?" He sent a knowing glance at me. "It's white noise until you focus and then it's like being invisible in the middle of a private conversation. But now that I'm back to normal, I don't have that and I never thought I'd say this, but between you and me... I miss it."

"I thought it was normal," I muttered.

He chuckled. "No. It took some getting used to for someone who has never had any ability to speak of. I remember the first night. I was at Quantico with a training class and the noise drove me bat shit. Your brother hadn't given me any instructions on how to lower the thought assault from an overwhelming roar to white noise. Instead, he found my struggle amusing, but I can't blame him. I wasn't all that happy when everything I had transferred to Valerie."

"I bet." I wouldn't be very comfortable with someone depleting my powers, either. Although, I wasn't sure of the realm of gifts I possessed. I just knew it felt like a ball of pure energy at the center of my body that snaked through every membrane of my form, creating a constant hum in my skin.

We both got quiet, and I watched the green scenery pass.

"Why me?" I asked as I turned the conversation over in my head.

"Why what?" he asked as we approached a scenic bridge overlooking a water way.

"Why do I have these... powers?"

He shook his head and shrugged. "I don't know. I think your mother was naturally blessed, along with your older brother, but their powers didn't really trigger until your mom met your father." Steve navigated from the high-speed lane to the right-hand lane, slowing down a little. "You were born out of that union of love and power and because of that, you're unique in ways a lot of us can't comprehend." He glanced at me and then set the blinker, taking the exit ramp. "In some ways, your uniqueness reminds me of Grace."

I lost focus on the conversation, studying the quaint town we drove through, and the glimpses I had of the water on a few of the curves. Steve pulled down a side road and approached a large home surrounded by a black iron fence and an immaculately manicured lawn. The fence looped around both sides of the house, blockading the residence from the bordering properties until it met up with a low stone wall and the water beyond. It was an impressive piece of oceanfront property.

Steve pressed the remote attached to the visor and the gates slowly opened, leading to a short driveway and a three-car garage. "This is your home," he said and something about the way he stressed the word your pulled my gaze to him. He stopped and turned off the car before meeting my gaze. "Your parents left it to you. We've been living here with you since you were nine years old."

"Oh," I said, and stepped out of the car when he did. The house was quiet when we entered. The garage attached to an open family room-kitchen concept that was warm and inviting. Beyond the sitting area stood sliding glass doors and an enviable view of the ocean. I crossed to them and stared out at the large, pristine pool. It all looked inviting and utterly foreign.

"Did you want to see your room? I'm sure your swim trunks are still in the drawers somewhere," Steve said, and the thought of jumping in that water turned me on my heels. I followed him up the stairs and we turned to the left. Steve showed me where the bathroom was and across the hall, he opened the door to what he said was my bedroom.

I stepped inside, hoping for some reference of familiarity and it just felt strange. Pictures on the shelves clearly contained me in them, along with some of the people who had come into the room yesterday. I picked up one of Tom and me, leaning together in formal attire, our champagne glasses raised, and grins plastered on our faces.

"Tom's wedding," Steve said when I turned to him. "You two had a little too much to drink."

I put the frame back on the shelf and picked up another one with three pictures. The center was a man in a suit who looked a lot like me and a stunning woman in a white dress. On one side, the woman stood with four children and on the other; the man sat with two boys on his knees.

"My parents?" I stuttered and got a nod in response.

"You remember them?" The hopeful arch of his brow hit a nerve, and I put the picture back on the shelf. It was a nice-looking family, but I didn't have any recollection of them.

"No. I look a lot like my father," I replied, pointing.

"Yes, you do." He stepped closer and pointed to one of the older children. "That's your brother, Eric. He was my partner at Quanitco. And that's Emily, your older sister. I never got the chance to meet her."

I stared at the picture. "Only Tom and I are alive?"

"Yes." He sighed and opened the top drawer of the bureau under the shelf of pictures. "Your swim trunks are in here. I'm going to enjoy the rest of the afternoon by the pool." He crossed to the door. "I'll bring my tablet out and we can start re-learning how to read and get you some basics of sign language so you and Tom can communicate."

"We talked just fine yesterday," I said, glancing at him and tapped my temple.

"You may have heard him without an issue, but he struggled to understand you, so having the sign language as a backup will help him. He can't read minds."

"Oh," I said, and he left me standing in what should have been a comfortable room, but I just wanted to be with Valerie, not here, feeling empty and lost.

Chapter 27

THE SUMMER HEAT HIT me when I stepped out on the patio. I crossed to the chairs and took a seat on the lounge chair next to where Steve's things were stacked. He was in the pool swimming laps. I squinted, scanning the oceanscape beyond the rock wall.

A tablet sat on the table between the chairs, and I picked it up, swiping my finger across the screen like Valerie had with my chart. It came to life, and I stared at all the icons, unsure of what to do next. None of the symbols meant anything to me and instead of trying to figure it out, I placed the tablet where I picked it up and lowered the back of the chair, closing my eyes in the warmth of the sunshine.

Pain gripped me, and I sat up with my breath ripping at my chest. Steve pulled himself out of the pool. Concern traced the lines in his face and his sharp gaze was locked on me. I glanced around the empty backyard with my heart pounding in my throat, not understanding the panic that overwhelmed me.

"Are you okay?" he asked, approaching me.

I shook my head, afraid to speak. My gaze continued to dart around, like I expected a monster to appear from the shadows.

"Just take a deep breath," he said and sat on the end of the adjoining chair.

I did as he said, and my head cleared.

"Take another breath," he said when I glanced at him.

Fragments of my dream surfaced, and I winced, shrinking into the chair at the intensity.

"You fell asleep," he said, and I nodded.

"Nightmare," I whispered in my broken way. The scratchy fear in my voice flipped the irritation switch. "I'm okay. Just thirsty," I said, forcing my muscles to relax.

Steve reached over the side of his chair and opened a cooler. He handed me a bottle of chilled water and I sucked it down, the coolness quenching my thirst and calming my nerves.

"You might want to jump in the pool to cool off."

I couldn't argue with his offer, and I drained the bottle before I approached the pristine water. The breeze ruffled through my hair, and I closed my eyes, letting the wind dry the layer of sweat on my skin. Before I jumped into the pool, the sliders opened, and a woman stepped out. The smile that formed warmed me. It took me a moment to place her name and then Steve filled in the blank without knowing it.

Jennifer. Steve's wife and, by default, my mother. She crossed the distance with a tentative gait, and I turned toward her instead of the welcoming pool.

"I'm glad you're home," she said, looking up at me, and then she stepped in and gave me a warm hug. "We've missed you," she said, and pulled away when I didn't reciprocate the hug.

"Thank you," I said and turned away, diving into the cool water. The chill of the water brought me to life, and I surfaced, shaking my head and flipping my wet hair out of my face. It refreshed in a way that soothed my hot nerves.

I climbed the ladder to the edge of the pool just as the rest of the crew came rolling out the door. Tom gave me a wave, and I sent a nod of acknowledgement in his direction. The quiet of the backyard erupted into activity, and I found a towel and dried off before the chaos got to me. I excused myself and headed into the house.

"CJ?"

I stopped with my foot on the first step and glanced at the door. A man filled the doorway, and I couldn't recall his name, but he was the man Grace had run to at the hospital.

"I never got to say thank you," he said.

I had no idea what to say, so I just nodded and headed upstairs without another word. In the bedroom, I slipped on dry shorts and turned on the laptop on the desk and picked up the piece of paper Valerie had given me just before I left the hospital. She had drawn the instructions of how to call her using the computer and I followed the pictures, plugging in the symbols on the keypad in the order they were drawn. The program buzzed, and I waited.

When her picture filled the frame, I exhaled and closed my eyes, hanging my head with the overwhelming relief.

"Hey. Are you okay?" her tender voice caressed me.

"Yes." I opened my eyes to her beautiful face. "I just miss you."

She glanced down at the desk in front of her and then back at me. "I miss you, too," she said and folded a notebook closed.

When she stretched, I just wanted to wrap my arms around her, and I shut my eyes. When I opened them, I stood in the room right behind her. The image on the computer was an eerie version of me, with a layer of milky white over my naturally bright eyes. Even with my non-existent memory, I knew this was not normal.

Valerie turned towards me and stood, running her hands up my chest with eyes filled with wonder. She grinned and wrapped her arms around my neck, pulling me to her lips. The sweetness of the kiss drew my breath from my lungs, and I was the one who broke free first. I traced her face with my fingertips and met her gaze.

"What the hell am I?" I whispered, looking between her and her computer screen.

"You are a very special man." She cupped my cheek, running her thumb gently over my lips before meeting my gaze.

I laughed softly. Special? This was more in the land of a freak than I cared to understand.

"Whatever runs through your blood gave you the ability to recover. A normal human would not have come back from the amount of raw damage you were brought to me with. It scared the living daylights out of me. My magic healing infusions brought your body back from the edge of death, but you had such severe brain damage that none of the doctors thought you'd ever regain the ability for coherent thought, never mind the ability to speak again. I like to think I had a little to do with your being able to function, but I think it was more about your inherent gifts than mine." She reached up on her tiptoes and kissed me gently.

"Speaking is debatable," I stuttered, and she smiled.

"I'm on call right now, so you have to go back." She pointed toward the computer monitor.

"How?" I didn't even know how the hell I got there in the first place.

"Just release the connection. Let go."

I hesitated and then dropped my arms, stepped back, and closed my eyes. The sensation of being pulled overtook me and I opened my eyes to my room and her smiling on the computer screen.

"Now, do you understand why I wasn't as concerned as you about not being in Maine?"

I slowly nodded. "I can do that whenever we talk?"

She put her palm on the screen and I covered it with mine, staring into her swirling irises. "Not necessarily. Popping into a roomful of people wouldn't be cool, so you have to wait until I give you the all clear, okay?"

I saw her point and nodded, dropping my gaze to the floor.

"Chris, no matter how much physical distance separates us, you can always step across it. You know why?"

I shook my head.

"Because we're connected. Not only by this unnatural power we both possess, but by the depth of love in our hearts."

I couldn't help but smile. "That's the corniest thing I've ever heard," I said.

"Yeah, well, you're a real mind fuck." She grinned and for the first time since I woke up, I wasn't worried about whether or not I would regain my memory, as long as I had her by my side.

The End

Continue CJ's story with Angel Heart.

About J.E. Taylor

J.E. Taylor is a USA Today bestselling author, a publisher, an editor, a manuscript formatter, a mother, a wife, a business analyst, and a Supernatural fangirl. Not necessarily in that order. She first sat down to seriously write in February of 2007 after her daughter asked:

"Mom, if you could do anything, what would you do?"

From that moment on, she hasn't looked back.

Besides being co-owner of Novel Concept Publishing, Ms. Taylor also moonlights as a Senior Editor of Allegory E-zine, an online venue for Science Fiction, Fantasy and Horror, and co-host of the popular YouTube talk show Spilling Ink.

She lives in New Hampshire with her husband and during the summer months enjoys her weekends on the shore in southern Maine.

Visit her at www.jetaylor75.com to check out her other titles.

If you liked ANGEL GRACE, check out the rest of THE RYAN CHRONICLES:

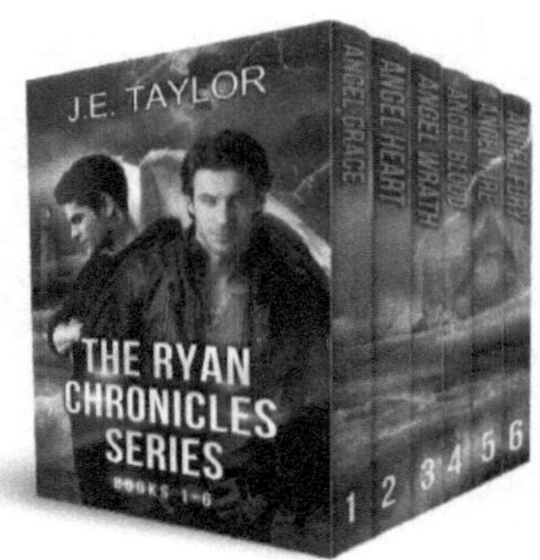

THE RYAN CHRONICLES

**Demons, vampires, angels, and the devil.
What the hell kind of nightmare do I live in?**

CJ Ryan was born with enough psychic power to destroy the earth. And Lucifer wants him to do just that.

Raised with a strong moral compass, CJ won't sacrifice innocent lives to protect his own, and that puts him at odds with the devil.

But if he doesn't give in, he and all he loves will become the target of Lucifer's rage.

When CJ gives his twin brother, Tom, a dose of his powers to keep him safe, it puts Tom directly in Lucifer's crosshairs.

As the final battle draws near, what will they have to sacrifice to keep their loved ones safe?

Can they survive the devil's wrath?

THE RYAN CHRONICLES includes these titles:

CJ's Story:

ANGEL GRACE - Book 1

ANGEL HEART - Book 2

ANGEL WRATH – Book 3

Tom's Story:

ANGEL BLOOD - Book 4

ANGEL FIRE - Book 5

ANGEL FURY – Book 6

Fans of Supernatural and Shadowhunters will
enjoy this series.

Find these titles and other fantasy and suspense
titles on J.E. Taylor's website!

www.JETaylor75.com